FORSAKING PARADISE

OTHER TITLES FROM KATHA

FORSAKING PARADISE

stories from ladakh

ABDUL GHANI SHEIKH

translated and edited by
Ravina Aggarwal

KATHA

First published by Katha in 2001

Copyright © Katha, 2001

Copyright © for each individual story is held by the author.

Copyright © for the English translation rests with KATHA.

KATHA
A-3 Sarvodaya Enclave
Sri Aurobindo Marg
New Delhi 110 017
Phone: 652 4350, 652 4511
Fax: 651 4373
E-mail: kathavilasam@katha.org
Internet address: http://www.katha.org

KATHA is a registered nonprofit society devoted to enhancing the pleasures of reading. KATHA VILASAM is its story research and resource centre.

Cover design: Geeta Dharmarajan
Cover and inside illustrations: Cynthia Hunt
In-house editors: Shoma Choudhury, Gita Rajan
Assistant editor: Anuradha Rajkumari

Typeset in 11.5 on 15.5pt ElegaGarmnd BT by Sandeep Kumar
at Katha and Printed at Pauls Press, New Delhi

ISBN 81-87649-16-X

2 4 6 8 10 9 7 5 3 1

Contents

INTRODUCTION

This book took shape one August evening, as I was waiting for a friend in her room in Leh, the capital town of Ladakh. The room was a blend of contemporary and traditional decor, with a square bed, fragrant incense sticks, blue, dragon carpets, and coloured scarves hanging from whitewashed walls. A wooden chogtse carved with the eight auspicious Buddhist symbols stood in one corner, upon which was placed an object that evoked much veneration in Leh then – a typewriter that my friend had lugged all the way from Bombay. I was sitting as I had many times before by this typewriter, contemplating ways to translate the chaos of my experiences into a coherent anthropological thesis, when I heard a knock on the door and in stepped Abdul Ghani Sheikh with a request for us. Could we type an application addressed to the District Commissioner, he wanted to know, for rehabilitating families who had fled their villages and were living like refugees in Leh without a roof over their heads? I did not need to question him about the reasons for their flight. Those were the days when frustration against the State government had manifested in a social boycott between the Buddhist and Muslim communities of Ladakh. Between 1989 and 1992, people were displaced from their villages, interreligious marriages forbidden, business relations suspended, friendships severed, and the streets of Leh deserted after dark. My friend and I typed the letter and took it to him.

Years later, when I began translating Abdul Ghani Sheikh's stories from Urdu into English, this incident came back to me, reminding me that in a land which borders Pakistan, Occupied Tibet and the Kashmir valley, where Buddhism, Islam and even Christianity have found homes, where the expanding international tourist industry is rivalled only by the economic presence of the armed forces, where the Ladakhi, Urdu, Tibetan and English languages compete to represent the culture, literature too takes on forms that are political and even paradoxical.

Situated between the Himalayan and Karakoram ranges in the state of Jammu and Kashmir, Ladakh is India's northernmost district. Until the mid-nineteenth century, it was ruled by monarchs who traced their descent from the tenth century Tibetan king, Skyid de Nyima Gon. Buddhism had a large impact on the art, architecture and literature that prevailed during these times. Writings ranged from subjects like logic and astrology to medicine and poetry. Dandin's *Kavyadarsa*, the seventh century Sanskrit treatise on the theory of poetry, translated into Tibetan by Sakya Pandit, strongly influenced the compositional and stylistic aspects of poetry.[1] Adaptations and transformations of the Indian epics, Ramayana and Mahabharata, were popular themes in literary writing.[2] Yet most of the literate intellectuals were monks and therefore the inclination in literature was towards the philosophical and spiritual side. The eleventh century translator, Lotsawa Rinchin Zangpo, and the sixteenth century founder of Hemis monastery, Stagsang Raspa, were among the scholars famous for their contributions to Ladakh's cultural and literary heritage.[3] In this pre-colonial Ladakhi society, live performances and oral forms of expression were more prevalent than scripted ones. The epic of King Gesar of Ling was enacted in private households as well as in public spaces. Artists known as manipa performed scenes from biographies of religious figures (nam-thar) and from the Jataka tales about the past lives of the Buddha.[4] Besides, the folklore of Chang Thang, Purig, Baltistan, 'Brog-yul, Sham and other Ladakhi areas had distinct regional, social and aesthetic characteristics that were not necessarily religious in content or style. However, there did exist some lay writers who composed fictional works. In Tibet, for instance, a nation with whom Ladakh shares a long cultural ethos, the minister of Domkhar, Tshering Wangyal, authored a classic novel in the mid-eighteenth century called gZhon nu zla med kyi gtam rgyud (The Tale of the Peerless Prince). Crafted in a style that blends prosody with prose, this novel is replete with incidents describing courtly intrigues, filial duty, ordeals of exile, and the triumph of spiritual truth. Most of the dialogues are written in verse, imbuing the linguistic conventions of Sanskrit poetry with a Tibetan flavour and context.[5]

In 1834, Ladakh was conquered by Zorawar Singh, general of the Dogra king, Maharaja Ghulab Singh. The British sold the Kashmir territories to the Dogras but retained control over economic affairs, especially over the lucrative trans-Himalayan and pashmina trade. This historical moment was to drastically alter Ladakh's fortunes. The roots of ecclesiastic and monarchic power were shaken and the extensive patronage once extended to Ladakhi language and literature was to end forever. During this colonial period, a new kind of literature came to dominate the landscape. Tools of modernity, such as census records, economic statistics, area maps, and land surveys, were deployed by imperial agencies for documenting the region.[6] Missionaries wrote "secular" and "objective" histories to rescue Ladakh from what they perceived to be the dark constraints of Buddhist ignorance while travellers and enthusiasts, describing the natural and anthropological terrain, were influenced by theories and tropes of truth-telling that prevailed in the Western imagination. At this time too, a systematic bid was made to grasp and translate the Ladakhi language. Missionary scholars translated the Bible into Ladakhi with great determination and prepared schoolbooks for the propagation of Christian values. The Moravian missionary, August Herman Francke (1870-1930), an avid enthusiast of local history, folklore and customs, published the first newspaper in Ladakhi, *La-dvags-gyi-ag-bar*. He is also noted for lobbying for a language that was the combination of colloquial and classical Ladakhi in order to reach a wider audience. Earlier, Francke's predecessor, H A Jaeschke, had assembled a Tibetan-English dictionary in 1882.[7]

The authoritative and realist style of the colonial period was occasionally undermined by the very props that authors used to make their accounts authoritative, a subversion most prominent in the semi-fictional narrative, *Drogpa Namgyal*, written in 1940 by Samuel Ribbach, a Moravian missionary commissioned to convert the recalcitrant natives of Khalatse village to Christianity.[8] This biography begins as an exercise of faith in the benevolence and civilizing mission of Christianity but gradually comes to reveal confusion and doubt as the priest's convictions and desire for control are confounded by his reluctant admiration for native beliefs.

In local writing too, biographies of religious figures were produced, spurred by directives from eminent scholars such as Tshultim Nyima, the founder of Rizong monastery, and Lobsang Tshultrim Chophel of Rizong, an artist, song writer and essayist.[9] Josef Gergan, who is best remembered for writing a history of Ladakh, also collected folklore, published texts on Christianity, and worked with missionaries on translating the Bible.[10] But by and large, literature was unavoidably affected by the new power structure with which it was forced to converse.

In the period after 1947, the face of Ladakh changed in significant ways. The wars with neighbouring Pakistan and China resulted in the redefinition of its territorial boundaries, altered modes of trade and learning, and gave rise to a highly visible military presence. With the construction of highways and roads linking Ladakh to other parts of India, travel increased on all fronts. Now tourism is one of Ladakh's largest revenue generators. The administrative bureaucracy that took root during the colonial era has strengthened, providing jobs, but also bringing about the reconstruction of all facets of life. The growth of markets and educational, information and media services has had a large impact on the manner in which knowledge is structured and defined.

Two major trends can be noticed in the literature of the

post colonial decades. In the early fifties, Ladakhi, also known as Bodhi, was accepted in the state educational system although it is still not recognized as an official national language. During the first phase following independence and in the aftermath of the 1961-62 Sino-Indian war, there was a surge of writing in Ladakhi devoted to the cause of nationbuilding, to the celebration of freedom and democracy, to the patriotic heroism of the defence forces under the threat of communism, and to modern notions of progress and development, especially in educational reform. Thus, Tashi Rabgyas wrote about Jawaharlal Nehru and Republic Day and contributed songs to build the morale of the army when China invaded India. Abdul Ghani Sheikh wrote a biography of Mahatma Gandhi in Urdu. Jamyang Gyaltsen authored a play about the virtues of martyrdom. Skits were staged to entertain military troops. Tashi Rabgyas applauded the virtues of the socialist democratic system versus extreme ideologies like capitalism and communism and declared that it was this system of government that was most congruous with Buddhist ideals. Of course, besides the official front, Ladakh's relation with the Indian state was debated and there were many dissenting voices. The internal factionalism in politics was reflected in controversial publications like *Ladakh Aazadi ke Baad* but over all these remained rather clandestine ventures.

The second post-Independence period, commencing in the late seventies, has witnessed much disillusionment with the promise of development. Rapid changes in lifestyle are experienced as a breakdown of traditional values and a loss of identity. Rather than national reconstruction, there are urgent attempts to renew a sense of pride in Ladakh and salvage what remains of its unique history and environment. Drama clubs and youth theatre organizations that were inspired by the Lamdon Youth Society, founded in 1969, presented morality plays in villages to eradicate social evils.[11] Often, the money they raised was used to renovate monasteries and promote cultural activities. At one time, songs extolled modern education as the light of illumination, such as Tashi Rabgyas's composition, "These days people roam in space on rocket horses. These days people try to walk on the moon. Little children of Ladakh, learn to read and write!" But now, the refrain "A, b, c slob, ka kha ma phang" (Learn your abc but don't discard your ka kha) sung by the famous artist, Phuntsog Ladakhi, reverberates in the Indus valley. Angchug Kidar and Angchug Ralam, representing the younger generation of musicians, recite with caustic dryness couplets about the advent of a modernity in which Madonna can be found in Ladakh and antiquated Ladakhi paintings are smuggled into foreign countries ("Thang-ka chi-rgyal la leb, Madonna nang la leb"). Even as the search for Ladakhi identity is emerging as the dominant trope of the times, the realization has set in that there is perhaps no unified Ladakh and that ethnic, religious and regional differences cannot simply be wished away. Even as religion is less likely to be upheld as the centre of cultural and intellectual experience, religious segregation is widening the chasm between social classes and communities.

As questions of identity and lifestyle are debated and contested, the adoption of an appropriately representative language for Ladakh has also become a volatile subject with enormous political overtones.[12] Despite pressure from political representatives, Ladakhi has not been recognized as an official national language. Attempts to revive interest in and reform the language have often met with harsh criticism. For example, during the fifties, Eliyah Tshetan Phuntsog, a popular leader, tried to reform Ladakhi by simplifying the spelling system. He targeted *a chen*, one of the two letters "a" and recommended eliminating it from the Ladakhi alphabet on the grounds that it was superfluous and that the *a chung* (small "a") was more efficient for everyday use. Tshetan Phuntsog, who had converted to Christianity, composed Christian plays and poems in Ladakhi modelled on traditional genres.[13] But opponents accused him of harbouring anti-Buddhist sentiments because the *a chen* is used as a sacred letter, as in the mantra, "Om Mani Padme Hum."[14]

Today, some of the educated literati ardently subscribe to the ideology that knowledge of classical texts is a must for the survival of a Buddhist Ladakh that they believe is threatened by modern life and border controls that prevent access to centres of learning in Tibet. Jamyang Gyaltsen, Nawang Tshering, Lobzang Tshewang, and Tshewang Rigzin from the Central Institute of Buddhist Studies are pioneers in the teaching of classical literature. Jamyang Gyaltsen has been instrumental in literacy operations undertaken by the literary society of Ladakh, the Ladakh Cultural Forum. He authored a book of grammar called *brDa sPron Nor bu'i rGyan* (The Jewel Ornament Grammar Book) in 1984, *Sherab sGron me* (The Flame of Knowledge) in 1995, and participated in the production of the two volume *Rig pa'i sGo* (Instructions to the Teacher) used by the State Resource Centre of the University of Kashmir for adult education classes in 1988. Jamyang

Gyaltsen's articles on Buddhist art, culture, and philosophy have appeared in *Ladakh Prabha*, a publication of the Central Institute of Buddhist Studies. His book *Rig Shung sNa Tsog Chunpo* (Anthology of Different Literary Forms), written in 1982, and his plays, *Sengge Namgyal* (1977) and *Yul Don la Rang sog* (Martyrdom) in 1987, all won awards from the Jammu and Kashmir Academy of Arts, Culture and Languages.

A second view in the language debate calls for embracing a more secular but standardized Ladakhi with a substantial fusion of Tibetan phrases and grammatical structures lest Ladakhi become incompatible with the religious canon and with Tibetan, Bhutanese, Sikkimese, and other Himalayan languages. This form of Ladakhi is used in the annual digest, *Lo 'khor gyi dep* and the journal, *Sheeraza (shes rab zom)*, both published by the Jammu and Kashmir Cultural Academy since 1976 and 1979 respectively. Contributions to the journals include academic and researched articles on subjects ranging from economy, literature, and social customs, to the history and art of Ladakh. The Jammu and Kashmir Cultural Academy was established in 1969 by Sonam Yakub.[15] It sponsors seminars for the dual purposes of conserving and collecting folk literature and advancing new writing for which experts are invited to participate from both near and distant regions of Ladakh.

A third view, forwarded by intellectuals attempting to construct a lexicon that is more accessible, is that language should represent contemporary social realities. These intellectuals use modern genres of writing, novels, poems (tshoms), and short stories (sgrung-bdus), to represent topics like corruption, tourism, caste, class, and education. For instance, the poet, Konchok Phanday, opens his anthology, *Phan bde'i legs bshad zhi bder dga' ba'i snying nor bzhugs so*, by offering the reader "The garland of the wish-fulfilling gem of the elegant sayings arising from the ocean of super-wishes of Phanday (myself), to the necks of peace lovers. Please tie it forever and ever as the ornament of precious wealth for a happy mind."[16] This bejewelled gift of verses, however, is presented with a cautionary and pessimistic note, "Even now as I put them into book form, I have not used too many fancy words or hyperbole. It is common knowledge that we Ladakhis are not fortunate enough nowadays to be able to study our own invaluable ancestral language or literature which dates back thousands of years and is on its last legs today."

Tashi Rabgyas, perhaps the best known writer, philosopher and historian of Ladakh, has tried to propagate the use of a simple language, without metaphoric ornamentation, so that it can be more inclusive of the popular community even though he himself is extremely well versed in classical and literary Ladakhi and Tibetan, to the degree that he is often mistaken for a monk. He has written several articles and poems, compiled a book of one hundred and twenty eight Ladakhi folksongs, published a collection of songs called *Teng sang gi glu* (Songs of Today), and a widely read history of Ladakh called *Mar yul La dvags kyi sngon rabs gsal me long zhes bya ba bzhugs so* (History of Ladakh Called the Mirror which Illuminates All) in 1984. Tashi Rabgyas regards himself as a "meddlesome man" whose objective is to arouse social consciousness with his words. He holds that classical forms should be known but change is also desirable. Simplicity can also be aesthetic. In the past, old songs were sung in different dialects but there was a beauty of expression in their diverse styles. Tashi Rabgyas's knowledge of Buddhist philosophy influences his ideas about the act of writing which, according to him, is a process of interdependence between writer and audience where verses sung with the right tone and inflection can inspire a poet to compose more lyrics whereas when they are distorted and taken out of context, they can cause the poet to regret the composition entirely.

Songs, stories and poems aired on radio have reached out to a large body of Ladakhi listeners, literate and illiterate, even in the most remote of areas. The All India Radio station in Leh, inaugurated in 1971, has been a creative outlet for several established and upcoming writers, heightening the demand for Ladakhi literature.[17] Nowhere has the mood of the times been captured so strongly in Ladakh as in oral poetry and songs where experimentation with aesthetic form is much more visible. Composers like Morup Namgyal have worked to rekindle an interest in literary and folk forms by revitalizing folksongs and by reciting and dramatizing epics like the saga of King Kesar of gLing. Morup Namgyal has also produced serials inspired by theological themes like *Dawa Zangpo* and *Lhamo Ithok* as well as plays with modern story lines. Modern play writing received an impetus in the fifties under the tutelage of Geshes Eshay Tondup who was rewarded with the "Robe of Honour" by the Cultural Academy.[18] In addition to the Jataka and nam-thar plays, dramas depicting historical events also have a place in Ladakhi writing, for example, Jamyang Gyaltsen's *Sengge Namgyal* in 1977 and Gelong Thupstan Paldan's *Tag pa Bum lde* in 1978. Tshewang Rigzin's *Tus kyi Ka chad* (Time will Tell) written in 1979 and Thupstan

Paldan's *La dvags ltas te 'grul* (Moving Forward with Ladakh in Mind) in 1982, deal with social change and development.[19] In recent times, experimental plays have been composed by Mipham Otsal, a graduate of the National School of Drama in Delhi, who insists that modern literature does not necessarily mean an abandonment of tradition. Otsal has fused methods from Greek and other Western theatre styles with traditional devices of nam-thar classics in his plays, *Lhamo Idthok* and the musical, *Nga'i Mi-tshe* (My Life), a story of the trials of three friends who attempt to win the love of a young mute girl whose silence spans lifetimes of loss and anguish.

Despite the developments listed above, there are those in Ladakh who allege that language reforms do not go far enough. That literature remains alienated from everyday life.[20] Correspondingly, a radical reform measure in Ladakh is the effort to institute phal skad or colloquial Ladakhi as the medium of instruction and basis of literary expression. *Mig gi gra mag* (A Splinter in the Eye), written in phal skad by Tshewang Toldan, a semi-autobiographical story about a boy, hated in his hometown, who gets an opportunity to expand his vision of the world through education, is one such example. The novel won the Best Book Award competition sponsored by the Cultural Academy in 1980. A romance novel, *Dzom skal* (An Auspicious Meeting), written by Tshewang Toldan in 1981 in phal skad was serialized in *Ladags Melong*, an English and Ladakhi bilingual journal, and his new novel, *Spal ba'i rimo* (Lines of Destiny) is under publication. The author also works as a newsreader and translator for All India Radio, Leh. His literary attempts have received some criticism for being grammatically challenged but he believes that although one should aspire to higher standards of writing, phal skad is vital and not opposed to yig skad (language of letters) or to chos skad (scripture).[21] The Buddha himself preached in Pali. Common speech is the only way through which lay people can understand religious teachings.

The premise that secular, spoken forms of Ladakhi will pave the way for the future is also the rationale for the Operation New Hope project, started in 1994 as a joint venture between the State educational board and a nonprofit organization called Student's Education and Cultural Movement of Ladakh (SECMOL). Here, the argument is not merely for the elimination of class or regional disparities but for the very survival of the Ladakhi language itself. According to the project's director, Sonam Wangchug, "When religion has taken a back seat in modern life, then just shouting the slogan of classical literature cannot redress the language issue. An education that only trains one to read complex texts like the Kangyur and 'Bum is as alienating as Urdu and English. Why hug your language so close to your chest that you smother it? For regional relations with Bhutan and Tibet, one needs a classical orientation but a mother whose child has diarrhoea also needs to be able to read the remedy that is presented in the secular literature. Not to do so is to miss the full potential of the language."

Operation New Hope seeks to reform the education process in Ladakh, contending that the three language formula recommended by the Education Commission of 1964-66 has worked to the disadvantage of the mother tongue and led to a confusion of languages and high dropout and failure rates among Ladakhi youth. The programme proposes the substitution of and eventual erasure of Urdu as the medium of instruction through a three step progression, where children start out by learning their home language in the primary grades. These are the colloquial dialects spoken in the different regions of Ladakh – Nubra, Leh, Sham, Chang Thang, Kargil. The next phase entails the mastering of a more standardized Ladakhi in order to lay the foundation for acquiring classical, religious, and literary education. Under this plan, it is English that will finally serve as a medium of instruction. Urdu and Hindi will be third language options. SECMOL has plans to produce numerous new textbooks, relevant to the particularities of Ladakhi society. The English primer, *Razia and Angmo* that they crafted in 1996 is one such example of the new textbook style.

At present, Urdu is the state language of Jammu and Kashmir. According to Abdul Ghani Sheikh, Urdu was bestowed to the state by the Dogra administration.[22] It was under the Dogra ruler, Maharaja Pratap Singh, who came to the throne in 1885, that Urdu was given the status of official language in the dominion. Until then, Persian was the official language, spoken largely by the elites. Urdu was used for routine office affairs as a link language between Tibetan, Punjabi, Turkish and Kashmiri traders and also as a means of communication by British officers who came to Ladakh for hunting and vacationing. In 1885, a school opened in Leh by the Moravian missionaries, taught both English and Urdu. In 1888, Urdu became the judicial language in the province of Jammu. It was only in the second decade of the second century, however, that the courts in Ladakh and the Kashmir valley adopted

Urdu. Around the same time, Urdu began to be used in the revenue system. In 1892, the Dogra rulers opened schools in the towns of Leh and Skardo in which Urdu and English were included in the syllabus. Soon after, English was excluded as the second language and Bodhi was taught in its stead in Ladakh.

Urdu newspapers began arriving in Leh during the second and third decades of the twentieth century. Among the initial consignments from Srinagar were *Inquilab*, *Milap* and *Pratap* after which *Sadaqat* and *Hamdard* arrived. Reading these newspapers, writes Abdul Ghani Sheikh, a Ladakhi called Munshi Abdul Sattar joined the Independence Movement and even went to prison for the cause. He was the sole freedom fighter from Ladakh. Munshi Sattar wrote a history of Ladakh in Urdu that was banned by the State government. This is one of the first books to be written in Urdu in the region.

Urdu was declared the medium of instruction in government schools on the recommendations of the Sayiddin Committee in 1940, during the rule of Maharaja Hari Singh. The Dogra administration took considerable interest in the promotion of Urdu. Maharaja Hari Singh appointed school inspectors for the advancement of Urdu and sponsored a number of awards and honours for Urdu writers.

After 1947, Urdu flourished in Ladakh. Several books were written in it and the number of Urdu readers reached thousands. In 1956, the Jammu and Kashmir government established Urdu as the official state language. Leh had a vibrant Urdu literary circle and poetry gatherings were attended by poets such as Khalida Bari, Munir Ahmed and Ruqia Banu. Today, Kacho Sikander Khan, Baba Abdul

Hamid, Zainul Abideen and Abdul Qayum are among the well-known writers of Urdu. Kacho Sikander Khan is renowned for his *Kaddim Ladakh* ("Ancient Ladakh"), a history of Ladakh and Baltistan, and for his annotated translation of the Ladakhi epic *Norbu Zangpo, Idthok Lhamo* into Urdu for which he was awarded the Uttar Pradesh Academy Award. Babu Abdul Hamid is a poet who writes in Ladakhi and occasionally in Urdu and has just published a trilingual dictionary with Ladakhi, Urdu, and English meanings for Ladakhi words. Famous Ladakhi writers like Tashi Rabgyas, Tshewang Toldan, Tashi Phuntsog and Stanzin Wangchug have published articles connected with Ladakh in the Urdu journal, *Hamara Adab*. Tashi Rabgyas, for instance, acknowledges the influence of Urdu writers, particularly the poet Ghalib and the Progressive Urdu writers in Kashmir who stimulated him by their commitment to egalitarian and socialist principles.

Both Urdu and Hindi were made compulsory subjects until the tenth standard when Sheikh Abdullah became chief minister in 1975. If a student were to study Hindi in primary school, he or she would have to learn Urdu as a secondary language from the fourth standard and vice versa. The administration passed this rule but did not take effective steps for its implementation. Of late, the Central Government has intensified its promotion of Hindi in Ladakh by sending delegates, posting signs in the airport and inscribing Hindi along with English and Urdu on official placards. With Urdu favoured by the State government and Hindi and English by the Centre, Ladakhis are not unjustified in calling for greater recognition for their own language. Some efforts to preserve

Ladakhi were made after the sixties when language reconstruction became one of the major imperatives of the Indian nationalist agenda, spurring linguistic data collection and textbook production. Sanyukta Koshal's books, *Conversational Ladakhi* and *Ladakhi Grammar,* were part of the integrative effort by the Central Institute of Indian Languages to create a resource for learning Ladakhi as a second language.[23]

Within Ladakh, opinions on what should be the standard language are further divided by the fact that Buddhists largely use the Bodhic/Tibetan script for writing Ladakhi while Muslims use the Urdu/Persian script. Both communities stress the importance of their scripts for deciphering and transmitting religious texts. But some Muslim scholars have recognized the problems of transcribing Ladakhi into Urdu. Commenting on the new compositions and genres in Kargil, Kacho Sikander Khan writes in his book, *Ladakh In the Mirror of Her Folklore*, "The progress thus made in the field of Balti Hymns is really an achievement. But the replacement of folklore and folk literature is an excess likely to cause a setback to secular literature with consequent loss to the community."[24] For that reason, the Kargil Social and Cultural Organization has attempted to revive folksongs and reclaim the Ladakhi script under the label, ngati skad (our language) rather than Bodhi, to popularize it in a fashion that is not identified with Buddhism solely. Similar affirmations of multiple cultural identity and ancestry have also been articulated in Baltistan where a number of intellectuals and educated youth are beginning to learn the Tibetan script and recover local traditions and customs.[25]

Ghani Sheikh supports the view that Ladakhi is the mother tongue of Ladakh and should be taught primarily and seriously in school. However, for pragmatic and social reasons, he is more cautious about the instant abandonment of Urdu. Socio-economic changes, development policies, and globalization have generated a need for Urdu and English as link languages.[26] Ghani Sheikh believes that it is important to write against communal segregation in whichever language one adopts.[27] According to him, "[A] language has no religion. It cannot be imprisoned within geographical borders. Urdu is a creation of the cultures of the Rivers Ganga and Jamuna. It is a combined heritage of the cultures of the Indian subcontinent and a symbol of communal harmony. Crores of people write and speak it and it has international recognition. Its easy and mellifluous nature charms everyone."

This anthology too is compiled of stories originally written in Urdu but it should be considered as an example of modern Ladakhi literature. Those generations of Ladakhi authors educated in Urdu have tried to shape Urdu with experiences that are explicitly Ladakhi. Urdu has given the Ladakhi language several words that have become part of it and has itself undergone a considerable metamorphosis in Ladakh. Although it may have been formally embraced by the bureaucratic workings of colonial governments, Ladakhi writers have altered this language in innovative ways through hymns, ghazals, and stories to create a medley of styles. For example, *Ju Ju Salam aalig*, a romantic duet in Ladakhi, composed by Tshewang Dorje, was a huge success not only for its entrance into the forbidden domains of romance but also for its provocative title which is an amalgam of Buddhist and Muslim greeting phrases.

Cultural hybridity is a crucial aspect of Abdul Ghani Sheikh's heritage too. He belongs to the Argon group of Muslims, descendants of Kashmiri and Yarkhandi traders who had settled in Ladakh and married locally. In his adolescent years, Ghani Sheikh read magazines like *Ratan* and composed his first poems. It was in 1953, after matriculation, that he authored his first story while working as a veterinarian stock assistant in Srinagar. Raised in a family with sparse financial means, he was unable to pursue his education through formal institutions beyond the tenth standard but his thirst for knowledge led him to persevere. He graduated privately and obtained a master's degree in history by correspondence. His mother told him that a Punjabi merchant had once brought some desserts to their home and reading Ghani Sheikh's horoscope, prophesied that he would one day be a scholar and carve a distinct path for himself.

Through his fiction, Ghani Sheikh has attempted to clear such a path, moving away from moralistic genres of literature to compose narratives like luminous mirrors that allow society to contemplate and transform its image. The "mirror" (melong) is a recurrent symbol in Ladakhi literature, where good writing is supposed to represent the truths of the phenomenal and transcendental world with crystal clarity. Ghani Sheikh feels that fiction weaves together truth and lies and therefore succeeds as an effective and acceptable mirror. He is conscious of the manner in which his own background is reflected in his writing. Having experienced poverty himself, Ghani Sheikh is not just a detached social observer but a writer who envisions his art to be striving for the realization of an egalitarian society.

As a young man, he was impressed by socialism and motivated by reading Progressive Urdu writers – Krishen Chandra, Ismat Chugtai and Manto, and European writers – Dostoevsky, Gorky, Tolstoy and Maugham. But even as he writes about epic subjects such as the horrors of Partition, Ghani Sheikh brings to Urdu writing a Ladakhi-styled prose, which reveals everyday acts of violence and heroism with such subtlety and simplicity that it may mistakenly be interpreted as facile by some readers. Living in a multi-religious society, Ghani Sheikh's stories have characters from both Islamic and Buddhist groups. With psychological intuition, his stories probe the social problems of common people coping with a world in which justice is not always the outcome of action. His writing is pragmatic and ironic, tinged with realism and attentive to twists of circumstance.

Besides his creative works, Abdul Ghani Sheikh is also recognized as one of the foremost scholars of Ladakh. He has written with passion and insight on subjects ranging from literature, history, philosophy (on Hegel and Nietzsche) and comparative religion. He has worked as a schoolteacher, screenplay writer and journalist. Among his books are two collections of short stories, *Zojila Ke Aar Paar* (On Both Sides of Zojila) published in 1975 and *Do Raha* (A Fork in the Road) in 1993, a biography on the famous Ladakhi pioneer, Sonam Norbu, a historical novel called *Woh Zamana* (That World Gone By) in 1976 and *Dil Hi To Hai* (It's Only the Heart, After All), a romantic novel which won the Jammu and Kashmir Cultural Academy's Best Book Award in 1980. His non-fictional books, *Ladakh ki Kahani* (The Story of Ladakh) and *Kitabon ki Duniya* (The World of Books), won second and third place respectively in a state competition held for the Children's Centenary Year in 1986.

The stories in this volume address some of the modern dilemmas of Ladakhi society. They reflect its composition and organization, its family structure, its caste stratification, and class divisions. "Hopes and Desires," for instance, unveils the aspirations of a poor girl as she prays for deliverance from her impoverished life only to realize the plight of those who are subject to greater oppression. Here, the audience is made aware of the discrimination suffered by those labelled as low caste (rigs ngan). Blacksmith, musician and mendicant castes are stigmatized as impure groups. They are often prohibited from inhabiting the same social space as high caste aristocrats (sku tags) or common folk (mi mangs).

Reconstructing history is also a dominant theme in a number of the stories. The reader is presented with an alternate reading of the life of Ghulam Rassul Galwan, whose autobiography, *Servant of Sahibs*, is the first text in English by a Ladakhi writer.[28] The author acquired economic and social standing by accompanying expeditions as a caravan leader and guide. Colonial travelogues highlighted the heroism of European visitors as they captured the wilderness and tamed the insurmountable Himalayas, underplaying local support and often complaining about the unreliability of porters. In contrast, Rassul Galwan's autobiography foregrounded his own bravery, selfless service and cultural sophistication without which the missions could not have been accomplished.[29]

Portraying Rassul's anguish as he must break the news of his departure to his family members, "Tales of an Adventurous Traveller" critiques the racial, gender and class politics of travel. Male wanderings for adventure or economic necessity often demanded emotional and material sustenance from wives and mothers who stayed home and remained unidentified in travel memoirs.

Perhaps the most powerful narratives in this collection are the ones that reveal the trauma of fragmented families and friendships and the suspicion and paranoia that comes to taint the relations between different religious communities. In "The Locked Trunk," a child's view of military and state rituals provides a commentary on the absurd mechanisms of colonial and national power. The tragedy is that emotions of camaraderie are locked away and lines are drawn in a way that two friends become confined to opposing sides of the Indo-Pakistani border. Despite this eerie fracture, however, a glimmer of hope for a story of collective healing and overcoming divisive boundaries remains ever present. The grandmother character of "Abhiley" who has no desire for life outside the safety of her village home is particularly important in this period of communal tension because she bears testimony to the sense of identification that Muslim households have felt with their Ladakhi homeland.

Changes wrought by development are recurrent themes in Ghani Sheikh's writings. Some of his stories depict a hopeful future where courage and honour prevail amidst corruption, greed and hunger for power. Others are sombre commentaries on the consequences of modernization. They portray, without nostalgia, the erosion of honesty as large scale dam works are erected, as culture is commercialized and the past turned into an object of fetishism by an expanding tourist industry whose desire for authentic experiences of Ladakh's landscape inevitably harkens the conversion and loss of those very environments.

The story, "A Forsaken Paradise," from which the title of the book is drawn, illustrates the clash between tradition and modernity, between two generations of male leaders developed from both secular and sacred cultural icons. Traditionally, renunciation as a means to liberation and enlightenment was a dominant model in Ladakhi literature. The renouncer gave up worldly pleasures for spiritual pursuits and often abandoned individual family bonds to cultivate compassion for humanity at large. In the modern period instead, it is the man that is materially successful and immersed in worldliness who commands respect from society. The chasm between the two generations seems insurmountable as each holds the other responsible for the cultural and familial erosion of the present day. The father returns from years of meditation only to find a Ladakh that he cannot recognize. The son who has awaited his father's return despairs that the father cannot serve as a guiding model for him. They cannot live together. The wisdom of the past has deserted the present. The father must forsake his son once again. But the impossibility of this father-son union is perhaps offset by the presence of another pair, that of the eager young tour guide and the old friend who hint at a middle path that requires appreciation and understanding from both generations. Paradise is an illusion or a temporary resting place, the story suggests. The quest is for a society that accepts, tolerates, and welcomes difference.

Through the ages, many writers have written eloquently about Ladakh, moved by its breathtaking beauty, lyrical panorama, and rhythm of life. The region is often romanticized as a utopian paradise where people live in harmony with nature. Activist networks have praised Ladakh's Buddhist culture for being a haven of alternative and sustainable ecological practices. Travelogues convey the impression that Ladakh is still an idyllic niche that needs to be saved from modernity. Political and cultural reform movements within Ladakh have also accentuated cultural conservation. But the metaphor of "paradise" imposes its own constraints. Opinions that convey resistance and plurality, that stand for different religions, languages, or class backgrounds, often get lost in the clamour for authenticity and purity. So it may be time to abandon the paradise analogy and look instead at the immense richness and varied realities of Ladakhi society. This is a moment in time when Ladakhis are seriously contemplating what the future holds for them. There is no consensus on the subject of modernization. Some find joy in the promise of the present. Others are despairing and see only ruin and stasis. And still others admit that there is much to grieve about but they are filled with hope that all is not lost, that the land is not forsaken by the onslaught of unfamiliar cultural trends. Writers and artists in Ladakh are searching for new idioms and symbols to breathe life into the expressive arts. They are in dialogue with the nation and the world around them. They are rising to meet the challenge of forces that would relegate them to the periphery of centres of power. New directions are beckoning them now. New winds are raging across the mountainside.

The process of making writing from Ladakh available in English has demanded careful and difficult choices. Problems with translation are rooted in histories of colonization, domination, and segregation. The relative prominence accorded to English in India has meant that Urdu and other regional literatures face inadequate readership as they are often not considered financially viable for publication. Translating from a regional language into English makes it more accessible to a broad spectrum of Western and English speaking readers from other parts of the world but it can also function as a unilateral form of appropriation. It has certainly been the tradition in Ladakhi, during its heyday of cultural patronage, that works of literature were translated into Ladakhi from different languages. Among its well-known translators were the Zangskar Lotsawa, Phagspa Sherab, his disciple, Wangchuk Tshultim, who was born in Baltistan, and Lotsawa Rinchen Zangpo, the eleventh century scholar from Guge, whose followers are credited with building one hundred and eight monasteries, including the spectacular one at Alchi. In recent times, the Constitution of the Cultural Academy of Leh has expressed its commitment to translated works.[30] Accordingly, Helena Norberg-Hodge's popular critique of development, *Ancient Futures: Learning from Ladakh,* was translated into Ladakhi by Tashi Rabgyas. Tashi Rabgyas has also translated the state laws of Jammu and Kashmir and a Natar Puja drama by Rabindranath Tagore. *Vasilisa, the Beautiful*, a collection of Russian folktales, was translated into Ladakhi by Tshewang Toldan as *mrZes ma lbe si li sa* and published by the Cultural Academy in 1994. Tshewang Toldan has a keen interest in translation and his new anthology of translated folktales from various parts of India is under publication. Other translations into Ladakhi include a Leo Tolstoy story translated by Morup Namgyal for the radio. In turn, Ghani Sheikh's stories too have been translated into Hindi and Telugu. Still, more efforts need to be made to ensure that the benefits of translation are channelled to literacy and literary movements, especially for encouraging writing and learning in local languages.

Translating literature is also controversial in a culture where the acquisition of literacy has not been the prerogative of the masses. Privileging written forms can come at the expense of oral performances and local ways of expressing culture. A large number of women in rural areas, for example, do not write texts but instead transmit biographical and cultural information about themselves through songs and poetry. One such oral genre is the skin-'jugs, soulful laments performed by brides at their weddings. Writing in Ladakh tends to be male dominated, even in more urban settings. Only a handful of women are published writers. These include Tashi Tshomo and Yangzin Dolma, teachers whose essays and poems have been printed in *Sheeraza*.[31]

Nevertheless, despite these limitations, the large amount of written scholarship that exists in Ladakhi and Urdu is rich and deserves attention. Ladakh has been receiving considerable national and international coverage making it all the more imperative to take note of writings by Ladakhis themselves.

This anthology could not have been possible without the collaborative efforts of Angchug Ralam, Bashir Ahmed Wafa,

Jamyang Gyaltsen, Kacho Sikander Khan, Konchok Phandey, Master Sadiq Ali, Mipham Otsal, Morup Namgyal, Nasir Hussain Munshi, Nawang Tshering Shakspo, Phuntsog Ladakhi, Sonam Angchug, Sonam Phuntsog, Tashi Rabgyas, Tashi Tshomo, Tshewang Toldan, Thupstan Paldan, Zainul Abideen and Achey Amina's warm hospitality. Monisha Ahmed, Agha Shahid Ali, Frederique Apffel-Marglin, Robbie Barnett, Brinda Bose, John Bray, Kai Friese, Kim Gutschow, Cynthia Hunt, Maya Ismail, Nicole Mailman, Ali Hussain Mir, Raza Mir, Rebecca Norman, and Ronald Schwartz opened up numerous possibilities with their comments and support. I owe many thanks to Christopher Wheeler for his editorial suggestions.

I have been fortunate to have the opportunity to work so closely with Ghani Sheikh on this project, consulting him on all changes, soliciting his opinion about words and ideas. We began these translations with "The Wind," a tale inspired by the social atmosphere of the boycott years. Ghani Sheikh wrote it shortly after our initial meeting in 1990 when he had asked me to type the housing petition. The original and translated versions of this account have had an uncanny moment of convergence. Over time, we have read this story at seminars and conferences. The last time I was invited to present it was at a symposium organized by various Ladakhi youth associations to promote a spirit of tolerance and harmony across linguistic, religious and regional divides. It is to this spirit that our book is dedicated.

Ravina Aggarwal

NOTES

1   See Roger Jackson's "Poetry In Tibet: Glu, mGur, sNyan ngaga and Songs of Experience," and Leonard Van der Kuijp's "Tibetan Belles-Lettres: The Influence of Dandin and Ksemendra," in Jose Cabezon and Roger Jackson eds., *Tibetan Literature: Studies In Genre* (Ithaca: Snow Lion Press ,1996).

2   Beth Newman, "The Tibetan Novel and its Sources," in Jose Cabezon and Roger Jackson eds., *Tibetan Literature: Studies In Genre* (Ithaca: Snow Lion Press, 1996) 411-421.

3   Nawang Tshering Shakspo, "Ladakhi Language and Literature," in C Dendaletsche and P Kaplanian eds., *Ladakh, Himalaya Occidental: Ecologie, Ethnologie. Recent Research in Ladakh 2.* (Pau: Acta Biologica Montana 5, 1985) 199-206. Thupstan Paldan, "The Language and Literature of Ladakh: An Overview," in Nari Rustomji and Charles Ramble eds., *Himalayan Environment and Culture* (Delhi: Indus Publishing Company, 1990) 256-262.

4   Nawang Tshering Shakspo, in *A History of Buddhism in Ladakh,* ed. John Bray (Delhi: Ladakh Buddha Vihara, 1988).

5   Beth Newman (1996).

6   Similarly, a critical analysis of colonial and Western literature on Tibet can be found in Peter Bishop's *The Myth of Shangri-La: Tibet, Travel Writing and the Western Creation of Sacred Landscape* (Berkeley: University of California Press, 1989) and Donald Lopez's *Prisoners of Shangri-La: Tibetan Buddhism and the West* (Chicago: Chicago University Press, 1998).

7   John Bray, "A. H. Francke's *La dvags kyi akhbar*: The First Tibetan Newspaper," in *The Tibet Journal* 13.3 (1988): 58-63; "A History of Tibetan Bible Translations," in Gudrun Meier and Lydia Icke-Schwalbe eds., *Wissenschaftsgeschichte und gegenwdrtige Forschungen in Nordwest-Indien*, (Dresden: Museum f|r Vvlkerkunde, 1990); "August Herman Francke's Letters from Ladakh 1896-1906: The Making of a Missionary Scholar," (Paper presented at the 8th Colloquium of the International Association of Ladakh Studies in Aarhus, Denmark, 1997).

8   Samuel Ribbach, *Drogpa Namgyal*, translated by John Bray (Delhi: Ess Ess Publications, 1986).

9   Thupstan Paldan (1990).

10   John Bray, "Towards a Tibetan Christianity? The Lives of Joseph Gergan and Eliyah Tsetan Phuntsog," in Per Kvaerne ed, *Tibetan Studies: Proceedings of the 6th Seminar of the International Association of Tibetan Studies, Fagernes 1992, volume 1* (Oslo: Institute for Comparative Research In Human Culture, 1994) 68-80.

11   Tshewang Rigzin, "The Place of Theatre in Ladakhi Literature," in *Lo'khor gyi deb,* 19 (1994).

12   Meanwhile, with the colonization of Tibet, the Tibetan language too was subject to political reforms. In the sixties, the communist regime modified the number of genitive particles in written Tibetan to advance its rhetoric of class equality and to facilitate the spread of revolutionary information amongst the masses, according to Tsering Shakya, "Politicisation and the Tibetan Language," in Robert Barnett ed, *Resistance and Reform in Tibet* (Bloomington: Indiana University Press, 1994) 157-166.

13   John Bray (1994).

14   Tshetan Phuntsog's language crusade was also interpreted as a covert metaphor in a game of political ascendancy over his nearest rival where he had positioned himself as the underdog, the *a chung*, implying that two leaders or two letters "a" could not exist in the same space.

15   Nawang Tshering Shakspo (1985).

16   Lama Konchok Phanday, *Phan bde'i legs bshad zhi bder dga' ba'i snying nor bzhugs so* (Here is the Elegant saying of (the Cause of) Benefits and Bliss, the Most Precious Wealth of the Peace Lovers) (Leh: Melong Publications, 1994).

17   Sanyukta Koshal (1979); Thupstan Paldan (1990).

18   Nawang Thsering Shakspo (1985); Thupstan Paldan (1990).

19   Jamyang Gyaltsen, "*La dwags su slos gar byung tshul*" (The Origin of Theatre In Ladakh), *Sheeraza* 2.2 (1980-81): 37-42.

20   A similar sentiment underlies the "new" style of poetry, egalitarian

and popular, that has blazed a formidable trail within occupied Tibet. In his article, "The Heartbeat of a New Generation: A Discussion of the New Poetry," translated by Ronald Schwartz in 1999, Pema Bhum writes that this "new poetry" was pioneered by the poet Dondub Gyal. It is new in that it departs from the conventions of composition laid out by the Mirror of Poetics theory (snyan ngaag me long ma), challenging the system of metrics and advocating free verse. It uses short titles that are not didactic but open to interpretation, it creates a space for the use of spoken language, it seeks the understanding of human experience by journeying through the inner states of the poet's mind into nature and society that lie beyond the self but are deeply connected with it, it revels in aesthetics and tries to free itself from the constraints of political dogma and religious doctrines, its style is dynamic and its ambition is to tap the pulse of a living Tibet and thus pave the way for a radical form of self expression and self determination.

21 In his article, "Ladhakologie - est elle une science?" in Claude Dendaletsche and Patrick Kaplanian eds., *Ladakh Himalaya Occidental: Ethnologie, Ecologie. Recent Research in Ladakh 2* (Pau: Acta Biologica Montana 5, 1985), the French anthropologist, Patrick Kaplanian, has also made a case for the adoption of an orthography that resembles the spoken form.

22 Most of the information on the history of Urdu that I have provided here has been translated from Abdul Ghani Sheikh, "Ladakh aur Urdu," *Taamir,* 2.14 (1983): 52-60.

23 Sanyukta Koshal, *Ladakhi Grammar* (Delhi: Motilal Banarsidass, 1979) and *Conversational Ladakhi* (Delhi: Motilal Banarsidass, 1982).

24 Kacho Sikander Khan, *Ladakh In the Mirror of Her Folklore* (Kargil: Kacho Press, 1997) 250.

25 Tarik Ali Khan, "Little Tibet: Renaissance and Resistance in Baltistan," *Himal,* 11.5 (1998): 14-21.

26 For a good description of the impact of contemporary changes on the Tibetan language, see Lauran Hartley, "The Role of Regional Factors In the Standardization of Spoken Tibetan," *Tibet Journal,* 21 (1996): 30-57.

27   Abdul Ghani Sheikh, "A Brief History of Muslims in Ladakh," in Henry Osmaston and Philip Denwood eds., *Recent Research on Ladakh 4 & 5* (London: SOAS, 1995) 189-192.

28   Ghulam Rassul Galwan, *Servant of Sahibs* (Cambridge: W Heffer & Sons Ltd, 1923).

29   See also Martijn van Beek, "Worlds Apart: Autobiographies of Two Ladakhi Caravaneers Compared," *Focaal,* 32 (1998): 51-69.

30   Similarly, the Amnye Machen Institute, a non-government organization, was founded in 1992 in Dharamsala by Tibetans in exile, mainly for the dissemination and translation of secular literature, according to Heather Stoddard, "Tibetan Publications and National Identity" in Robert Barnett ed, *Resistance and Reform in Tibet* (Bloomington: Indiana University Press, 1994) 121-156.

31   For example, Tashi Tshomo, "Bu mo rnams gyi rgyan chas gos," (The Jewellery and Dress of Women) *Sheeraza,* 14.5-6 (1992): 79-89.

A TRUE PORTRAIT

The old man stood at the crossroads swirling his prayer wheel and chanting mantras. It was early in the morning. An American tourist, coming out of the hotel on the opposite side, saw him there and promptly drew out his camera for a photograph. "Rupee, rupee," the old man shrieked, waving his skinny arms in dissuasion. The tourist took a two rupee note from his wallet, slipped it into the old man's hand and proceeded to photograph him in different poses.

"He looks like a live specimen of ancient Ladakh and a true representative of its culture," said the tourist to the local guide who had just joined him. "Since Tibet became a prohibited area, we come to Ladakh to experience Tibetan culture and Buddhism. But all we see here is young people in jeans and jackets. I fear the culture of this place will be totally erased in a few years. In our country too, the Indians are losing their culture."

Taking a seat on a bus bound for the Hemis monastery, the American continued his monologue, "But our government is taking considerable measures to preserve it. You people must do something solid for that as well."

The sun's rays covered the crossroads like a carpet. It was an extraordinary sight. Tourist groups of different nationalities emerged from hotels nearby. Seeing the old man, they reached for their cameras reflexively. But he kept waving his hands and shouting, "Rupee, rupee." A group leader gave him a ten rupee note and immediately Minoltas, Yashicas, Canons, Fujicas, Roliflexes, Zesicons, and Zeniths began snapping away. As if he was an important dignitary or international VIP surrounded by press photographers.

Even though the old man was clad in traditional Ladakhi attire, it was his visage and demeanour that attracted the gaze of all those around him. Quaint objects dangled from his long, wide sash – a metal spoon, a leather needle case, a flint and a big key. Turquoise earrings hung on his ears and a grey rosary around his neck. Broken frames, tied by a white thread, rested on his nose. His face was wrinkled due to old age and he had a limp in his right leg. When he walked, his whole existence looked rather awkward.

Long ago, a local photographer had taken a snapshot of him, hundreds of copies of which had been sold to foreign tourists. Inspired by this, another photographer had printed coloured cards with his picture on it. These postcards were also in high demand. Tourists told all kinds of stories on the backs of these postcards. Some asked how their friends were faring. Some wrote descriptions of their journeys. A boyfriend used this picturesque card to write sweet nothings to his girlfriend. God knows to how many houses and destinations his photograph had travelled!

Every summer, when the Leh-Srinagar highway opened to traffic and tourists began arriving in Ladakh, the old man also materialized. When the roads closed and the traffic of tourists stopped, he too departed from Leh. No one knew of his whereabouts during the winter season.

The tourist market had created much competition among travel agencies and businesses but his somewhat unique style kept him in demand. His haunt, the crossroads, was on the slope of the path that led to the victory peak, Namgyal Tsemo. On this peak, stands Leh's highest monastery, built in the sixteenth century by King Tashi Namgyal to commemorate his victory over the invading armies from Turkistan. In the afternoon, when the old man stood there rotating his prayer wheel, cameras would start clicking around him. When the sun receded into the western mountains and the flow of tourists petered out, the old man would reach into the pockets of his long robe. Taking out notes of international currency, he would count them twice, fold them inside his shabby wallet, and place the wallet carefully in the inner pocket. Then, dragging his small frame with his good foot, he would walk down the sloping path.

At the other end of the path was a small tavern into which he would disappear. Confidently, he would take a seat on the rug. The woman in charge would welcome him and place a cup on a coloured, ornate table before him. He was a regular customer of hers.

After consuming many cups of chang, the old man would be floating on air and talking in a loud voice. The woman would fill his goblet with the barley beer again and again. After fifteen or sixteen cups, he would stop her from filling his empty cup. Pulling out the wallet from his pocket, he would give her two ten rupee notes. The woman would return three rupees and he would carefully put them away in his wallet. Soon, the prayer wheel would start slipping from his hands. The woman would pick it up and place it respectfully on the shelf.

When darkness fell, a man would arrive and lead him away. As if he was a blind man at the edge of a bridge with a handkerchief spread before him, who had to be steered home in the evening along with the alms pitying passersby had thrown his way all day.

One day, a Hollywood film crew came to Leh for some authentic shots of old Ladakh when Leh had been an important trade centre of Asia. The film unit summoned the old man. At first he was hesitant but when he heard of the two hundred rupees an hour remuneration offered, he acquiesced happily. Even in his wildest dreams he had not imagined that he would earn such a big sum for just one hour.

An old shrine in the Manekhang area behind the main market in Leh was selected for the shooting. A makeshift set of the marketplace was constructed. Traders of Turkish caravans bartered with Ladakhi vendors at one end while women sold vegetables on the other side. Stray donkeys and cows roamed about freely. Carrying a basket on his back and a prayer wheel in his hand, the old man was to circumambulate a chorten, a reliquary built by Buddhists for the dead.

A large crowd gathered around the chorten to watch the shooting. The surrounding rooftops teemed with spectators anxious to catch a glimpse of the beautiful Hollywood actress. The police found it rather difficult to control the crowds. It took over an hour to set up the camera and other equipment. All this while, the old man waited under the hot sun.

After some rehearsals, the camera began rolling. Voices shouted, "Silence! Ready!" An assistant cued the old man to begin walking. He lifted the big basket and walked around the chorten, turning the prayer wheel with one hand and a rosary with the other.

"Cut!"

A young man in modern clothes, watching the shooting from a neighbouring rooftop, had come within the frame of the camera.

The old man returned to his place. On receiving his cue, he began walking again. The camera rolled on but barely had half the circle been completed when there was a call to stop.

An object from the modern world had once again intruded the realm of the traditional. Two policemen were dispatched to the rooftops to prevent the spectators from surging forward.

The sun was shining hard. Once again, the director yelled, "Cut." Weighed down and weary, the old man's entire body was bathed in sweat. Never before had he experienced such hardship. Never before had he been made to work with such diligence. Once a Japanese television team had taken several shots of him but that had been smooth sailing. He wanted to toss the basket and run away but the prospect of receiving two hundred rupees an hour fettered his feet.

All the unit members were engrossed in work. Cut was called out six times.

"This will be the last shot," the director shouted for the seventh time.

The unit members became active again and there was much running about. Additional rookies were sent to the rooftops so that once the shooting started, the spectators would be prevented from moving forward.

"Silence!" came the director's command.

"Ten seconds, eight seconds, four, three, two ..." Receiving his cue, the old man stepped forward, turning the prayer wheel and rosary. He began circling the chorten. His feet were heavy and his steps extremely slow. He had barely completed half the circle around the chorten when his legs started shaking and he lurched to the ground, never to rise again.

The postcards with his photograph can still be seen in many shops of Leh and the tourists buy them with much enthusiasm.

"A True Portrait" was published as "Muqabala" in the January/February issue of *Al-Atash* in 1985. It was reprinted in *Bano* in April 1990.

ABHILEY

When Abhiley heard the news of the earthquake in Turkey, her face turned ashen. Choked with tears, she said, "Oh Protector, you are rahim va karim, so merciful and benevolent. Have pity on my granddaughter Rukshana. Keep her safe!"

All of us burst out laughing. Kaga, my elder brother, said, "Abhi, Rukshana is in Srinagar. The earthquake has hit Turkey which is thousands of miles away from Srinagar."

But tears rolled down Abhiley's sunken cheeks. It is not an easy task to cajole our abhi or make her understand. How can one explain that the world has nearly two hundred countries and that all places are not like our village with its mere forty, fifty houses?

She had become increasingly apprehensive since the evening Rukshana departed to Srinagar. The bus in which Rukshana was travelling had broken down near Kargil. Abhiley argued that if the bus had broken down, it must mean that Rukshana had not survived. To convince her otherwise, we had to use our eloquence to the utmost.

Kaga consoled her. "Abhiley, if the bus stopped working it doesn't mean that it has had an accident. Buses often break down during a journey. Sometimes the oil freezes due to the cold. Sometimes nuts and bolts of the engine don't function or a certain part stops working. The driver parks the vehicle on one side of the road, repairs it, and then the vehicle takes off."

We also had to take extreme precautions before commenting on the news in front of Abhi. The mention of daily happenings, like the rolling of a bus into a ditch at such and such place,

---

Abhi is the Ladakhi term of address for grandmother. The suffix, *ley*, is a mark of respect.

the derailing of a rail cart, the disappearance of an aeroplane, or the firing of a bullet at some procession or other was enough to trigger an interminable series of questions. "Is my Rukshana safe? Was Rukshana travelling in that bus? Rukshana is very curious. She must have gone to see that procession."

We would start laughing and Abhi would admonish us yet again for sending Rukshana to Srinagar. When she expressed her helplessness, we comforted her, saying that Srinagar is a mountain resort, that it's called Paradise on Earth, and every year thousands of tourists visit Kashmir to explore it. We tried to make her understand that Rukshana was in Srinagar not out of some desperation but to get further education and seek a better life. When we promised that next spring we would take her to Srinagar too, Abhi fell silent. If we had brought up the subject of her visiting Srinagar before Rukshana left, she would have risen in anger and pursed her mouth, declaring, "I won't leave my children and grandchildren to go anywhere."

Srinagar aside, our Abhi has not even ventured beyond a distance of ten miles from our village. Two years ago, after a gap of eight years, she had made it to Leh town for the annual Dosmoche festival, held every winter to purge the town of evil. She saw masked dancers and musicians leading a procession from the palace through the main bazaar. She came across monks burning effigies and making crosses of thread to trap harmful spirits and hungry ghosts of the old year. There was much hustle-bustle. But that evening, when Abhiley returned home, she could only complain, "Oh dear, my head is spinning. There were so many people there that the breath was squeezed out of me. I will never go again."

During those days, a daughter of a distant relative came to

visit us in our village. She lived in Delhi. Abhiley did not recognize her and kept staring at her. We stifled our laughter and enjoyed ourselves thoroughly.

Finally, when Abhiley was told that this was Dolma, she was astonished. "La Dolma, I was wondering from where this memsahib had descended upon our house. What kind of clothes have you put on?"

Dolma smiled.

"Where have you come from, Dolma?"

"I live in Delhi, Ama."

"Oh, then you must be meeting Rukshana every day!"

"Ama, Delhi is very far from Srinagar."

"Have you never met Rukshana?" Abhiley sighed in disappointment.

"I spent two days in Srinagar on my way here. I tried to meet Rukshana but couldn't locate her house, Ama."

"Oh, what have you done!" Abhiley was miffed. "You were in Srinagar and couldn't find the house of my granddaughter."

"It's a big city," my sister-in-law interrupted. "It has a population of five to six lakhs, Abhiley. How will people know where someone lives unless they have the complete address?"

"Everyone says the same thing." Abhiley's tone became serious and her eyes filled with tears.

I remember another funny episode regarding my abhi. I was very young those days. My uncle sometimes came to the village to hunt. Once, my uncle returned to the town but left his double-barrelled gun behind. Agu had kept his gun in the kitchen where a big battalion of children of various relatives and in-laws often gathered. Abhiley was so tense that she couldn't sleep for two nights. She guarded the kitchen all day to make sure no child touched the gun, convinced that as soon as it was touched, the bullets would explode instantly and everyone would die. She would have locked the door if it had been any other room, but how could she close off the kitchen? When Aba and Agu returned to the village on the third day and heard about the situation, they rolled on the floor with laughter.

I must confess that I take advantage of Abhiley's simplicity. The army of children always present at our home often tears my notebooks to make kites and boats, ripping the sheets to shreds with scissor-like fingers. I put on a tearful face before Abhi and tell her that these papers are official. If they are torn, I will be penalized. These words work like magic on her and she preserves my papers with such intense care that no child would dare to even look at them. Not stopping at that, she saves all sorts of scraps and titbits even when I am away and when I go to the village, she presents them to me. Among them are papers from the grocer and snuff-seller for wrapping spices and snuff.

All grandmothers, despite their varied backgrounds, are similar, particularly in their reaction to modern technology. Like one of the grandmothers in our neighbourhood. When she refers to an aeroplane, she switches to honorific speech. "The plane-saheb has arrived," "The plane-saheb must be facing a lot of difficulties," (on hearing it make noises) and "Today, plane-saheb was very big." They say that when another abhi saw a plane for the first time, she went to greet the plane with bundles of grass in her basket.

There is another episode associated with our abhi. She and

another abhi from our community went to see a film. It was their first film and will probably be their last one. With their weak eyesight the moving images on the screen held no more truth for them than a dream. They watched the film less and complained more of headaches and nausea. Shortly, with my elder sister's help, they understood that one of the important themes in the film was about a mother-in-law's harassment of her daughter-in-law. The next day saw both abhis sitting on the rooftops of their houses spewing venom on the mothers-in-law of the world. God save us from their wrath! Incidentally, a girl from our neighbourhood had been married into a household where she did not get along with her mother-in-law. So from then on, whenever anyone mentioned the film, the two abhis would immediately start rebuking all mothers-in-law bitterly.

The neighbouring abhi is of the same age as our abhiley. She is a frightening woman indeed. When she is annoyed, she roars like a lioness. She has her own style of relaying all matters ranging from politics to domestic tales. A few months ago, when I was leaning on the staircase, reading a book, I heard the two abhis telling each other their stories, the same everyday talks with which my ears were familiar. "Surely, it's an omen signalling that the day of judgement is near." They must have been referring to a fatal accident or to the simultaneous death of two men. Or "Demoness! Disgrace! Ignoramus!" all aimed at chastising a well-dressed woman.

During the conversation, the nextdoor abhi asked about Rukshana's well-being and before Abhiley could reply, she informed her that there were severe floods in Srinagar. I closed the book I was reading in dismay, and awaited Abhiley's reaction.

"La," screamed Abhiley. "Floods. Where did you hear this news, Hajira?"

"It was on the reldi yesterday." The nextdoor abhi always referred to the radio as Reldi.

"Wallah, no one told me about this."

"Didn't Bashir tell you?"

Abhiley sighed, "You don't know how my sons are."

After a few moments, she said, "I will go down, Hajira. My heart is thumping loudly." I heard the echo of her footsteps. Now calamity has befallen us, I thought and sped down, leaping across the stairs. The echo of Abhi's weak footsteps could soon be heard on that part of the staircase where I had been reading a few moments ago. As soon as she came down, she stormed at us, "Did I not say not to send Rukshana to Kashmir? But no one paid heed to my words."

"What's the matter?" asked Kaga.

"There are floods in Srinagar. Floods!" Abhiley waved her hands in agitation.

"So what?" Kaga was irritated. "It's a big city. Floods come. Storms come. Fires blaze."

"Enough, enough. I have heard enough." She placed both her hands on her ears. Her eyes brimmed with tears.

For several days, Abhiley's doubts did not abate and she became very quiet.

She decided to accompany Kaga and I on a trip to Srinagar. On the way, she was very uncomfortable with vomiting and dizziness. We spent the night in Kargil and reached Srinagar the next day.

Kaga said, "Abhi, you were worried about Rukshana. See how hale and hearty she looks. Her face is fair and her cheeks have turned red."

Abhiley clung to Rukshana and wept a lot. After resting for two days, Rukshana took her for a tour around Srinagar. "Abhi, look what a big and beautiful city Srinagar is! This is the Dal Lake. This is Nishad Bagh. These are the Shalimar Gardens. Nehru Park. Char Chinar ..."

Four days passed without incident. On the fifth day, Abhiley declared, "I will return to Leh. I miss the children. I miss my daughter Jamila. My granddaughter Halima. I miss little Javed."

She insisted on this in such a manner that on the very same evening we had to purchase return tickets to Leh for ourselves and our abhiley.

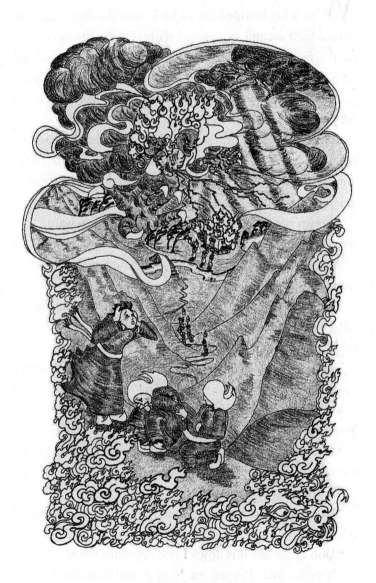

THE WIND

We climbed halfway up the mountain and stopped to rest by a big boulder. Dawn broke and the morning light draped itself around us. I looked at my village – the monastery on the mountain, the ruins of the old fort, the dilapidated school building where I had studied up to the fifth standard, green terraced fields, rocky pastures, and narrow paths on which we had spent so many days of joy and sorrow.

My gaze came to rest on our house, hidden behind the willows and poplars. Bundles of grass and cakes of dung were arranged neatly on the roof. Our cow was at the manger, eating grass. Our horse was tethered to a peg near the garden.

My eyes skipped to the small graveyard where my ancestors were buried. Tears filled my eyes.

Aba, I thought, We are leaving you behind and going away from this village. Not with pleasure but in helplessness.

I bade farewell in my heart, as though I was looking at my village for the last time. My wife's and daughter's eyes were moist with tears too.

We rested for a while and started walking again. Sonam's words were echoing in our minds. I remembered him knocking softly on our door two or three hours ago, and entering the house furtively.

He looked subdued. Squatting on the bare floor, he whispered, "Siddiq, I have bad news for you."

We stared at his face in alarm.

"All of you must leave this house and go," my close friend whispered.

"Don't joke like this now," I said apprehensively.

"It's not a joke. I'm serious. Now. At this moment. Leave!"

"Why?" I shouted.

"I don't have an answer for this Why at this time, Siddiq." A teardrop rolled down his cheek.

My wife and daughter began wailing. "What have we done wrong? What crime have we committed?"

"The fault is not yours or ours. This wind has blown in from the town."

"Who told you so?"

"Tashi. Dorje told Tashi. Tshering told Dorje. Tashi was saying that I should not disclose this to anyone else or these people will burn his house down."

"These people?"

"Yes. These people who have come from the town say that you must surrender one or the other. Your village or your religion! Siddiq, only humans bring such winds."

Sonam was behaving very mysteriously. We were astonished at the sudden turn of events. The villagers had always been kind to us, so what had changed? We had lived here for three generations. Far from any harassment, it was love that we had received from everyone. They had shared our joys and sorrows with such sincerity!

"I don't believe my ears, Sonam."

"If only it could be that way."

Then Sonam addressed my wife. "Achey, this is not the time to cry. Prepare to leave now." After a few moments, he said again, "Leave through the mountains, Siddiq, and make for the town."

"How shall we cross the mountains in this darkness?"

"It is dangerous to take the road," he warned us.

Sonam rose and disappeared behind the door. He had come in like a thief and vanished like one.

We made three bundles of our clothes, useful wares, my wife's jewellery, and packed some dry bread. We filled the manger with hay and fodder and tied the horse to a peg near the patch of grass in the garden. We placed grass in the pen for our sheep and goats and then crossing the stream, made for the mountains.

The yellow rays of the sun quivered over the peaks before the sun itself appeared from behind a mountain. We were only about a hundred and fifty steps away from the top when we heard the beat of drums and a sound like the buzzing of flies. Our feet were rooted to the spot. In a few moments, a crowd emerged from the grove in front of us. We managed to hide behind a boulder as the crowd marched forward and their slogans reverberated in the air. I felt as though strong gusts of wind were attacking us from all four directions. Sonam was right when he said that it was only humans who brought such winds.

Five decades ago, a gale had swept in from the town, bearing the smallpox epidemic. Several lives had been lost. Many houses had been destroyed. My abhi, achey, and nono had also fallen prey to this gale.

Then the cool, easterly breeze had come with the message of independence. Pleasant winds drifted into our land, spreading the light of education and bringing with it electricity and irrigation water. But *this* new current was entirely different. Poisonous, malignant wind! Never had such a wind blown into our village. It was even more menacing and toxic than the air that carried smallpox. That wind had taken the lives of people but had not separated humans from humans!

From the top of the hill we could see the crowd gradually

moving towards our house. Most of the people were strangers to me. Then, suddenly, I saw my neighbour Dorje in the crowd.

"Dorje!" I called out instinctively.

"Aba, look," my daughter shrieked. "Azhang Sonam is also in the procession,"

"It can't be true. Sonam would never come."

"Look closely, Aba. The man who holds the flag, who else is that if not Azhang Sonam?"

It was true. The man holding the flag was her Uncle Sonam.

"Look Aba," my daughter cried out again. "Azhang Tshering and Azhang Tashi are also there."

"Speak softly, Fatima," my wife admonished.

My heart sank at the sight of my close friends marching with the crowd.

The group stopped in front of my house and their provocative chants echoed in the mountains, creating a sinister atmosphere. I could see Sonam, Dorje, Tshering and Tashi raising their fists in response to every chant.

Most of the people in the procession probably thought that my family and I were hiding in the house. Many of them broke into it when no one emerged from inside in response to the chants. Among the intruders were Sonam, Dorje, Tshering and Tashi.

After some time, when these people stepped outside, they were carrying things looted from my home. Sonam had taken the gas cylinder and stove. Tashi was hauling the big copper pot the villagers used to borrow from me for all big feasts and celebrations. Dorje carried something under his arm. It looked like a carpet. Tshering cut the rope that tied the cow to the peg and drew it away. A man took hold of the horse. Two men released the sheep and goats from the shed and led them aside. One man stumbled along under the weight of our tent, another keeled over from the burden of a trunk.

I could not believe my eyes. My wife and daughter were watching this spectacle from their hiding place behind the boulder.

Had Sonam cried crocodile tears in front of us yesterday? Had Tshering, Tashi and Dorje played a trick to make me homeless? The world was full of betrayal and friends so disloyal, I thought in my heart.

I was searching for the answer to my questions when I saw smoke rising from a window of my house. Within a blink of the eye, the whole house was consumed in flames. Tongues of fire touched the skies. Darkness swam before my eyes. My wife screamed.

"Khuda ka shukr hai, Khadija, our lives have been spared," I uttered tonelessly.

Gradually, as the crowd dispersed, we left our hiding place and moved stealthly until we reached the summit. The sorrow had driven away all feelings of fatigue and hunger.

We finally reached the town the next day and saw several other refugees like ourselves. We had no further news of the state of our fields, gardens, grain or cattle. Links with our village were totally shattered.

Two months passed in this manner. One day, in the town, I saw Sonam approaching me. Hatred swelled in my heart as blood rushed to my eyes.

"What else have you come to take, Sonam?" I turned my face away as he came up to me.

"Siddiq, I regret that we could not save your house and all your possessions. We tried very hard to stop those people from setting your house on fire but our efforts were to no avail. But your gas cylinder and stove are with me. Tashi has your pot. Dorje has saved two of your carpets. Tshering is looking after your cow. That night, we went back quietly to your half-burned house. We recovered some pots and pans and two bags of grain, which we have kept safely. All these things with us are your possessions. We are waiting for the day when you will return to the village, my friend. My Angmo and Dorje's wife, Dolma, say that without Fatima and Khadija, the village seems desolate."

Was it the morning wind or the fragrant evening breeze? After a long time, I felt as if I was surrounded by clean air.

"The Wind" was published as "Hawa" in *Shama* in December 1998. A Hindi version appeared in *Sushma* in January 1999.

NAME

The late night show had just ended. I ran into him outside the hall as I walked into cold gusts of wind blowing all around us. A tanga carrying the last four or five viewers passed by. We were the only two left on the road.

"Where do you want to go?" he asked me.

"Ramnagar."

"That's where I'm going," he said. "Let's walk!" His voice had an air of command. His face was barely discernible in the shadowy darkness, wrapped as it was with a muffler to protect his ears from the cold.

"The film was total rubbish," he pronounced, without looking at me. "They have created some semblance of Hindu-Muslim unity. But when have these Muslims followed a straight path?"

What kind of a man have I run into? I wondered and repented my decision to walk home with him.

"These people devise some new ploy every day." He began coughing violently.

What a strange man, I thought to myself. He doesn't even know me but has absolutely no hesitation about voicing his opinions so openly.

"What, ji? You agree with me, don't you?" Without waiting for my reply, he continued, "If people want to stay in this country, they better behave like good citizens."

I resolved in my heart that if he asked me for my name, I would give him a false one. I would have to change my profession and my address too.

But he kept on talking. "They take their processions through Hindu neighbourhoods but if the Hindus take one through their area, they raise a big ruckus, hurl stones at the procession, throw acid, and raise fights about temples and mosques."

As he was talking, I chose the name Ramlal in my heart. I also chose an innocent sounding profession and changed my residential address.

"They don't participate in the national mainstream," I heard him say. "As a matter of fact, their eyes are still on Arabia and Iran. How can a film reform such people? What do you think?"

I did not reply immediately. For a few moments, my heart said that I should summon some moral courage and tell him that the film was very ethical, that it provided a lesson in unity to different communities. In the very next moment, however, my heart silently cautioned that it was not appropriate to argue with a stranger. I assessed him from the corner of my eye. His chest was broad and he was taller than I was. Surely, he would be stronger than me. I looked at his face, now partially hidden in the darkness. Two long, long whiskers grew from his lips. His eyes shone like glowing embers. Maybe he had a knife in his pocket. Maybe he would stick it into my chest in the dark of the night. I began trembling. The faces of my wife and children, hungry and anxious from waiting for me, swam before my eyes.

I need to reach home quickly, I told myself. But instantly a sign saying Coward popped up in front of my eyes. I reassured my conscience that it was foolishness to engage in an argument with an eccentric person. He was talking nonstop and I was murmuring in assent.

"But are Hindus any less?" He changed his tune now.

"They are also rascals."

Startled, I looked hard at his face. But it was inscrutable and expressionless. As usual, he continued talking without looking at me.

"These people commit crimes on minorities. The death of a person is no big deal for them but if a cow dies, they are ready to move heaven and earth. Sometimes, instigators kill a calf and throw its corpse into a well. Or steal an icon from a temple and then blame the Muslims for it. In the process, they taint their hands with the blood of innocents."

With a sigh of relief I reclaimed my name in my heart. I was once again a journalist who lived in … My conscience rebuked me for my earlier intention of lying but he was already muttering something else.

"Before advising Hindus on national integration, the minorities should be taught to live peacefully." He had changed course once again. "How long will the government keep changing its policies to woo Muslim votes? How long will the whims of minorities be tolerated?"

I was caught in a bind. I rechristened myself Ramlal and changed my profession and address once again. Suppressing my mental struggle, I assured my conscience that one should not injure the feelings of others. After all, courtesy too, is important. Why should I make this man uncomfortable by revealing my real name? The poor man was expressing the pangs of his heart. What had I to lose?

"How did you like the film?" he asked suddenly catching me unawares.

"I can't really say that it was good but it was not bad either," I was deliberately cautious.

"You are right," he nodded, still not looking at me. "As a matter of fact, it was just like our government." Now he began a commentary on politicians. "It is the politicians who instigate people and make them fight against each other in order to hold on to their seats. Ordinary people are good in their own right. They cut each others' throats influenced by the hollow chatter of these selfish politicians."

Then he began talking about social justice and human friendship. I felt like a true fool. My existence was swinging like a pendulum between true and false names, dividing my being into two selves. I was relieved to spot Ramnagar's bus station at a distance.

"You haven't said anything." His voice was soft.

"Because you were talking ..." I replied vaguely.

"Where do you live in Ramnagar?"

My heart thumped thinking he would now ask for my name and with it my profession and address. But once again, without waiting for me to answer, he began to vent the agonies of his heart. "If I could control it, I would pull out this government from its roots."

Madman! Eccentric! I abused him in my heart.

Just as we were about to part near the bus stand by the old mansion, he gripped my hand firmly. "You didn't even tell me your name."

"Ram Mohammed," Caught off guard, I stuttered in such a way that a confused, mixed-up version of my real and imaginary names flew from my lips.

"Pleased to meet you," he responded before I could correct myself. "I'm D'Souza. I teach philosophy and psychology in the college."

I looked at him in the light of the lamppost. There were no scary whiskers on his lips. Nor were his eyes like glowing embers.

"Name" was published as "Naam" in *Shama* in August 1981. Its Hindi version appeared in *Sushma* in 1981 and was translated into Telugu in 1981 for *Vipula*.

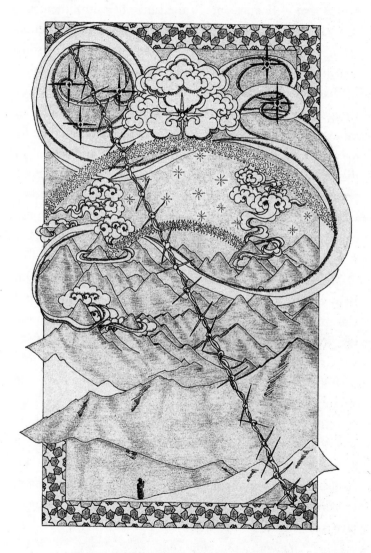

TWO NATIONS, ONE STORY

The Partition of India has affected more than just the destiny of a nation. It has split apart towns, villages and homes that were once one. At the Line of Control there are, they say, such villages where a brother can see his brother on the other side – ploughing the fields, watering them, harvesting and threshing the crops. But if he wants to meet his brother on that other side, he has to trek several kilometres from his village and cross the forbidding Khardong pass, eighteen thousand feet high, to reach Leh. From there, he can then fly to New Delhi. After several months of struggle and waiting in the capital, should he acquire a visa, he can travel to meet his brother in Islamabad or Lahore, but not in his brother's own village in the trans-Himalayan territories. In spite of being so close to his brother's home, he is so far away. Like a star in the sky which he can see but not touch.

My brother lives in Skardo, the biggest town of Baltistan. Before Partition, Baltistan was a province in Jammu and Kashmir. The chief administrator of the Dogra administration, the Wazir, spent the summer in Leh and six months of the winter in Skardo. His entire staff shifted from Leh to Skardo with him. Kaga Din Mohammed, my elder brother, was the Wazir's clerk.

In the year 1947, autumn cast a long shadow over Leh. Hindustan was divided and the new nation of Pakistan appeared on the world map. Uncertainty prevailed around us. As usual, Kaga accompanied the last Wazir, Lala Amarnath, to Skardo. I was young those days. The dim picture of Kaga's face still swims before my eyes. Before leaving, he had presented me with a one anna coin.

A year later, Skardo was conquered by Pakistan and Kaga

became a resident of that place forever. He was not alone. There were other Ladakhi government employees trapped there. Even today I can remember a few of those names – Munshi Ghulam Mohammed Tak, Khoja Mohammed Iqbal, Munshi Abdul Hamid, Sonam Tshering, Sonam Tashi, Munshi Abdul Salam. Initially, they all lived in the hope that they would soon be released and reunited with their near and dear ones. On this side too, we hoped that some avenue would open for their return. We would assure Ama and our sister-in-law, Achey Saffiya, that Kaga would return soon. In this manner, two years passed.

At first, there was no channel for sending letters. Sometimes, news would trickle in that Kaga was faring well. Then, gradually, correspondence started between the two nations. Good and bad news was exchanged. The first one to receive unhappy tidings was Munshi Ghulam Mohammed whose wife had passed away in Leh. Munshi was alone when the letter arrived. No one was present to give him consolation or sympathy. Tearfully, he searched for his friends to tell them what had happened. After this tragedy, they made a pact amongst themselves not to receive private letters directly. For the postman, Munshi Gulam Mohammed Tak now became Munshi Abdul Hamid, Din Mohammed became Khoja Mohammed Iqbal, Khoja Mohammed Iqbal became Sonam Tshering. Our missives became symbols of the anticipated grief that those exiled in Skardo would inevitably have to face. So they remained tense when letters arrived, afraid of receiving bad news from family members.

Occasionally, the letters contained happy tidings too. So and so had had a child, Azgar had secured the medical seat,

Anees had managed to get admission to the engineering college, Jamila's son had found employment, Tufel had built a new house, and so on. Letters from Kaga reassured our troubled souls that he was alive and well. One day, Kaga sent divorce papers to his wife, Saffiya, along with a long letter. He had written, "Saffiya, god knows if we shall ever meet again but the possibilities seem remote. I have been living the last six years with your memories, dreaming every moment of meeting you. But how long will you wait for me? I'm sending these divorce papers to you with a heavy heart. You are still young and beautiful. You will find a nice man to make you his life partner."

Approximately a year after this, Kaga sent another letter announcing his wedding. Sadly, the day we received his letter was also the day our father passed away.

The letter carrying this unhappy news to Kaga was received by Khoja Mohammed Iqbal. One day, Kaga saw from his window, a group of his friends approaching his house slowly. Why are they coming today, he wondered. They usually arrive together to felicitate for Id but today isn't Id. I'm sure they're bringing some unpleasant news.

His heart pounded heavily. By the grace of God, let my parents be all right, he prayed in his mind. His friends entered the house, led by Munshi Ghulam Mohammed. Kaga heard the news. What he feared most had come true.

A month and a half later, we received a letter of condolence. "If only I myself could come to Leh to share this pain," he had written. But Kaga was a government employee. The state of Jammu and Kashmir was a sensitive border area. It was difficult to obtain permission to visit Leh. I too was affiliated with the official media. There were the same obstacles preventing me from visiting Skardo.

Five years later, mother passed away and then one after another, aunts, uncles, and friends.

Then, one spring, when irises and hollyhocks bloomed in the fields of Leh, we received a letter from Kaga, joyfully announcing the arrival of a new guest in his house. Her name was Zakiya. Achey Zohra sent her greetings to all of us. When a year had been completed, Kaga sent news of another child. Her name was Zarina.

The letters stopped suddenly in 1965, when India and Pakistan went to war. The situation repeated itself after the war of 1971. When correspondence was finally resumed, we learned that Zakiya was studying in the tenth standard, that Zarina had passed the eighth standard examinations, and that two new members had appeared in the house – Fakhar-ud-Din and Mohammed Naim. Now, in the letters, came greetings and blessings from Kaga, his wife and four children.

From the beginning of time till the end, the cycle of births, marriages and deaths will continue for the survival of the human race. Our mother used to say, "Girls belong to others," so we were very happy to receive our brother's letter one day, informing us of Zakiya's wedding. As was the custom, there was an invitation card with it. Soon afterwards, Zarina also tied the knot.

The hands of time kept moving. Time passed. Days turned into weeks, weeks into months, and months into years. Then, thirty eight years after he had left, Kaga wrote to say that he would be coming to Leh. When we heard he had reached

Delhi from Islamabad, we prayed in our hearts that the weather would be clear the following day so that the flight from the capital to Leh would not be cancelled.

We reached the airport in three taxis filled with relatives and Kaga's friends. Excitedly, we watched the Boeing appear on the horizon and land on the tarmac. Kaga stepped into the arrival lounge. If we had not seen a recent photograph he had sent us in advance, we would have found it hard to recognize him. So many years had passed. He had left as a bridegroom and returned as a grandfather.

He was introduced to everyone. All of us became very emotional. We had tears in our eyes. What strange creatures humans are! We shed tears both in moments of pain and intense joy.

The taxi made its way towards Leh. "Leh has changed a lot," Kaga observed, looking at the houses on both sides of the street beyond the airport. "This place used to be totally deserted. People said it was haunted. They were afraid to walk here after dark."

"None of us could imagine, even in our dreams, that there would be residential neighbourhoods here," Kaga's friend added. Kaga had been hearing about the changes in Leh for a long time. Now he could see them with his own eyes. Changes had come to Skardo as well. During the last decades, electricity, running water, and films had come to both regions. Radio stations and colleges had been established in both.

Many people came to greet Kaga as soon as we reached home.

"Din Mohammed, do you recognize me?" a visitor asked. Kaga stared at him intently.

"You don't? I'm Ahmed Din."

With a cry of delight the two old friends embraced each other warmly.

"Is your brother, Amir Din, well?" Kaga asked, after the initial euphoria had settled down.

"He passed away six months ago." Ahmed Din's face held a deep sadness. "Din Mohammed, most of our friends are not in this world. Only Ghulam Sultan, Munshi Nabi, Stobdan, and Nur Din are alive."

"My heart used to mourn when I received news of death." Kaga rubbed both his hands in anguish. "I thought if only I had two wings. I would fly and come here."

"Allah be praised that we could see each other before our death," said Ahmed Din.

"Sometimes I feared, Ahmed, that I would not see Ladakh in this life again."

"This is Parvez Ahmed. He is an engineer." Someone introduced a young man.

Kaga stared at the young man blankly.

"He's the son of the late Akbar Shah."

"Oh! He was born several years after I left for Skardo," exclaimed Kaga. He addressed the youngster. "I had close links with your late father. I received the news of his passing away in Skardo."

A newcomer embraced Kaga and shook his hand. "You are Ghulam Rasool, aren't you?" Kaga asked.

"Yes, I am." Ghulam Rasool smiled. "You identify me correctly, Din Mohammed."

"You had two young children. Where are they today?"

"With your blessings, both are with me. Kadir is the father

of four sons. He is running his hotel. Akhtar is a contractor. He has two sons."

"Congratulations!"

"Now tell me, when will you visit us?"

"Inshallah, I will definitely come soon."

After Ghulam Rasool's departure, Kaga remarked, "His family used to be very poor, almost on the verge of starvation. Now he looks so affluent."

"He is very wealthy indeed," agreed Ahmed Din. "Both sons have good incomes. They also have two trucks and taxis."

"Things have changed a lot in the last thirty eight years," added Azhang Ghulam Sultan.

Kaga nodded. "In Skardo too, the situation is similar."

People kept coming to meet Kaga in search of information about their loved ones in Skardo.

Munshi, Ghulam Mohammed's younger brother, came for a visit and asked about his brother.

"He is well and has sent some letters and presents for all of you."

An elderly gentleman asked about a certain Abdul Khalid.

"I've heard he's in Karachi," replied Kaga. "We haven't met for the last fifteen, twenty years."

Sonam Tshering's father arrived and inquired about his son. "He's faring well," assured Kaga. "There is a village in Baltistan called Ganok. He lives there with his wife and children. Sometimes, he comes to Skardo to purchase things but I haven't seen him in the last three, four months."

"He must not have known of your visit to Ladakh?" The old man asked hopefully.

"No," Kaga replied, "He didn't."

"When are you returning?"

"I'm here for a while."

"Take a letter for me, please, and a gift."

"Of course. Bring them over someday."

The next day, Kaga said to me, "Ghani, take me to the burial grounds. Show me the place where Ama and Aba rest."

We went to the graveyard and he knelt before our parents' graves. For a few moments, his face was clouded with the grief of the whole universe. After thirty eight years, he had returned to his ancestral home only to face a strange, changed land. In his long absence, Aba and Ama had left the world. So many memories were associated with this place. Tears swam in his eyes and his lips quivered. I could feel the enormous internal struggle in his heart. Maybe he was telling Aba and Ama, I could not meet you in this life. I could not look after you in your sickness. You both raised me with love and nourished me so well but I could not fulfil my duty. How can I repay your favours? Forgive me. I was helpless. Otherwise, I would not have stayed away like this.

It hardly takes any time for a month to pass. Kaga's visa was about to end and he was anxious to go back to Skardo. He loved his new country where his children were and where his new relatives and friends lived.

We went to the airport to see him off. He took with him photographs of cherished ones.

"Now you won't find it difficult to obtain a visa. Come back soon with Achey Zohra," I said.

"First you should visit Pakistan with Amina."

With aching hearts, we all bade him farewell.

In 1995, just when Kaga and his wife were planning to come to Leh, to attend my son's wedding, Achey Zohra passed away. Then with the turbulence in Kashmir, correspondence between us became a little irregular. We received each other's letters only after a long time. We learned that several letters we had sent had not been received. In the beginning, we complained about not receiving replies but gradually we became aware of the situation and wondered in astonishment where these straightforward and simple letters disappeared.

Instead of sending letters directly to Skardo, I started handing over my envelopes to some European tourists requesting them to stamp it in their country and mail it to Pakistan. Ironically, these letters reached Skardo safely after travelling thousands of miles from London or Birmingham or Copenhagen or some other European city. And letters sent from Skardo, situated only two hundred and three miles away from Leh, disappeared mysteriously.

I have always wanted to visit Skardo. Not only because my brother lives there but also because Skardo has been a vital part of our heritage. Ladakhis who have visited both places, or those who know about the relations between the two regions, have a great desire to see Skardo.

Racially, culturally, and linguistically, the people of Baltistan and Ladakh are one. The disposition of their inhabitants is also very similar. The history and geography of Skardo and Leh bear striking resemblance. The surrounding mountains, the old palaces and the ruins of forts are still held together by fragments and relics of a long history, sometimes parallel, sometimes interwoven, never totally forgotten.

Baltistan and Ladakh were both independent states until the mid-nineteenth century, when they were conquered by the Dogras of Jammu. The Dogra administration constructed post offices in both places simultaneously in 1875. In 1892, primary schools were opened in both the towns. After twelve years, the primary schools were upgraded to middle schools. The population of both states was about four thousand before 1947. Now it is over twenty thousand each. Baltistan gave Ladakh butter, dried apricots, apricot seeds, and earthen pots and we gave Baltistan pashmina, wool, and salt. Baltistan gave Ladakh polo, musical instruments, and ghazals. Ladakh gave Baltistan songs and epics.

It is said that where there is a will, there is a way. During the month of August in 1995, a seminar was to be held in Islamabad under the aegis of the Pak-German Research Project and the Lok-Versa Institute on the cultural and geographical links between the Hindukush, Karakoram and Himalayan regions. I received an invitation to participate in the seminar on behalf of the Pak-German Research Project. The best part was that in the programme, a tour had been arranged to the northern areas, including visits to Skardo and Gilgit. I could not ignore this golden opportunity.

I deliberately did not notify my brother. I wanted to surprise him. One day, I imagined, I would suddenly reach Skardo, knock on the door of his house and say, "See who has come." He would be astounded to see me standing before him.

The director of the Jammu and Kashmir Cultural Academy in Leh, Nawang Tshering, was also invited along with me. We were both spared the excruciating wait in front of the Pakistani High Commission in Delhi. We were easily granted a visa to participate in the seminar and six of us from India reached Islamabad. But the Home Ministry of Pakistan did not permit us to visit Baltistan. A distinguished professor and historian of the Lok-Versa Institute and the Chair of the Pak-German Research Project made several appeals on our behalf but their efforts were not successful.

"My elder brother is in Skardo," I said to the Professor. "In the last forty five years, we have only met once."

"You will get a visa. You should write a separate application. This is a humanitarian matter, after all."

The Chairman said, "This is a case of two brothers reuniting after years. You will definitely get a visa."

But I did not get a visa to visit Skardo. The Director-General of the Lok-Versa in Islamabad tried to console me. "I had the same problem when I came to India. I had a desire to see the Taj Mahal but I was not given permission to go to Agra from Delhi."

Under the circumstances, the only instrument of surprise left for me was the telephone. I called my brother to inform him that I was in Islamabad and he came to Islamabad to see me. We were meeting again after seven years. Past memories rushed in. Zakiya had settled in Islamabad after her marriage. We went and met her husband and six children.

The scholars from India were invited to a dinner by the Indian High Commission in Islamabad. During the conversation, when I mentioned not getting permission to visit my brother, the First Secretary of the High Commission said, "Whether the Pakistani government gives you a visa or not, we will definitely give your brother a visa for Leh so you may meet him."

Several writers, historians, and intellectuals had come to Islamabad from Baltistan to participate in the seminar. Among them were two writers, Syed Mohammed Qazmi and Mohammed Yusuf Hussain Abadi, who had already been introduced to me as we had never met before. I had been corresponding with Qazmi for some time now. He had compiled and translated Ladakhi folk songs into Urdu, annotating them with historical backgrounds. Mohammed Yusuf had written a history of modern Baltistan.

For the seminar, my Ladakhi compatriot, Nawang Shakspo, and I presented papers that compared the cultures of Baltistan and Ladakh. On our last day in Islamabad, the Baltis threw a farewell party for Nawang and me. We recorded our feelings for each other on tape, hoping that they may be preserved for eternity. We also exchanged our books.

That evening, in Islamabad's President Hotel, I gave Kaga a letter for the First Secretary of the Indian High Commission. I wanted him to establish contacts for a visa to India.

The next morning, Kaga came to bid me farewell at the Islamabad airport. "Before dying, I wish to come to Ladakh once again," he said.

"You should make passports for your children too," I urged him as we hugged each other. "So that our children and grandchildren get to know each other."

With that wishful thought, I left for Ladakh.

The official story of our countries, India and Pakistan, written during the last fifty years, is filled with tension, hatred, malice, and misunderstandings. I believe that one day the story of how separated hearts are united again will also be told.

TALES OF AN ADVENTUROUS TRAVELLER

In the year 1895, after a hazardous journey of one year and three months in Central Asia and Tibet, Rasool Galwan and his companions arrived in the village of Thiksey. Another day's journey and they would reach Leh and be reunited with their family members.

"Tomorrow, at this time, we will reach our homes," said Razak Akhun. "Let us bake a cake each for our families. Our wives will think we have become used to eating sumptuous food on the trip and feed us well."

"Does your wife always serve you unsavoury meals?" Kalam Rasool questioned.

"My wife cooks tastier food than yours, Kalam."

"But mine cooks only after getting the recipe from yours."

"Why are you two arguing uselessly?" Hussain intervened. "Razak is right. If we take the cakes with us, our wives will think we were well fed during the trip."

Rasool Galwan, a famous Ladakhi adventurer and the leader of the caravan, was distressed. "You people are dreaming of food and I have not been able to sleep for the last two nights. Memories of the house I left behind keep flashing before my eyes." His companions fell silent at this and busied themselves with the baking.

That evening, a government representative from Leh arrived at their camp site. He shook hands with Rasool and said, "The Wazir has sent me from Leh for an audience with Littledale Saheb."

"Did Wazir Saheb get my letter?"

"Yes, he did. I hope you had no problems with the arrangement of horses from Chusod?"

"It was all right. Tell me, are my mother and wife in good health?"

"Yes, yes, they are fine."

May God make true what he says, Rasool prayed in his heart.

He couldn't sleep a wink that night. Like the reel of a film, incidents of the past rolled before his eyes.

Just a few years ago, Rasool Galwan and Kalam Rasool had returned to Leh from a long and perilous hunting expedition to Central Asia with two Britishers, P W Church and E L Phelps. Pleased with Rasool's service during the trip, the Englishmen had thrown a reception in his honour at the Wazir's garden in Leh. Representatives of the State and Cabinet officials had attended the reception. Placing a fine turban on his head and praising his services during the odyssey to the icy Mustagh Pass, P W Church had announced, "Rasool willingly risked his life for us. He is a popular singer as well. But above all, he is a nice man."

Flushed and pleased with the honour he had received at the reception, a happy Rasool had returned home to discover that his wife, Zubeida, had passed away in his absence. His companions had kept him in the dark about her death during the journey.

"I am very grieved by this news," a distressed Rasool had said to his mother. "When Zubeida was alive, I barely showed her any affection. Not that I was a philanderer either. Tell me, Ama, before she died, did she hold any grievances or misconceptions about me? Was there any dirt in her heart against me?"

"She remembered you fondly until her last breath, Rasool," his mother sobbed.

"Fate did not favour me. If only I had been by her side …"

Rasool had always been an enthusiastic dancer, singer and banjo player but after Zubeida's death, he had given up singing and dancing. His friend, Nono Sonam Wangdus, was perturbed by this. One of Rasool's benefactors, Khwaja Ghulam Rasool, counselled him. "We have had birth and death since the beginning of time. The flow of life does not stop with them." But Rasool was adamant.

"For how long will you torture yourself with the grief of Zubeida's death, Rasool? Please marry again," his elder sister had implored him after some time had passed.

"Achey, I do not wish to marry so soon. Memories of Zubeida come back to me again and again. When she was alive, I did not care for her much but ever since she has passed away, her picture swims before my eyes constantly. I just can't think of marriage now."

"But Rasool, you know she will not return to this earth again. Ama cannot manage the work alone. After marriage, you will also find rest."

His mother too had begged, "You choose a girl, Rasool, and we'll take the proposal. Khatoun, Fatima, Malo, Khanum — whoever you like, we will send a message to the family."

"No, Ama, I do not wish to marry now." Rasool had been firm in his decision.

"Sherab says that there is a very nice girl in Chushod. She is beautiful and of the same age as you. If you like her, we will send the proposal." His mother had insisted.

One day soon after that, Ama announced that a relative had spoken to the girl in Chushod and that she had accepted him.

"Without seeing me?" Rasool was astonished.

"She must have heard of your feats," Rasool's sister said.

"You must see the girl," his mother insisted again. "Her name is Maryam and she is from the Stakpa family. Her parents will accept the match. Next week, there is a fair at Shey. The girl will surely come to see the fair. You can see her then."

Rasool had not seen Zubeida before the wedding. He had married her on the recommendations of his mother and the middleman, Ghulam Rasool Khansama. This time, however, he and Kalam Rasool set off the following week for Shey, not very far from Chushod. They had little trouble identifying Maryam once they learned she was at the fair and Rasool fell in love with her at first sight. Maryam, however, remained oblivious of their stares and attention.

Kalam Rasool, who is famous for his romantic exploits and who has also been mentioned in books on caravan adventures, said at once, "What a girl! She is a nightingale of a thousand tales. If I were not married, I would have married her immediately."

On their return from the fair, Khwaja Siddiq Shah who was an important man of Leh, Rasool's uncle, Ghulam Qadir, and a female relative, proceeded to Chushod with the customary offerings. Maryam's family accepted the proposal and the wedding party returned from Chushod with blazing torches signalling their success.

Rasool invited about forty guests to the wedding. People from Leh came to watch the special events organized by Rasool's friends and fellow adventurers at a garden near his house. Kalam Rasool and Razak Akhun performed a sword act to the beat of damans and surnas, local drums and oboes.

Balti and Turkish dances delighted the guests. For the finale, they danced the Dragon and Amban dances learned from Kashgar. The same Amban dance came to be known as the Boat Dance in Leh later. These dances became so popular with the residents of Leh that they had to be performed without fail at all state and civil functions from that time on.

Barely a fortnight after the wedding festivities, Rasool said to his mother, "Ama, the Wazir is sending me to Kashgar to travel with a saheb."

"What are you saying, Rasool? How can you go so soon after your wedding?"

"This is exactly what I said to Wazir Saheb, Ama, but he insists on sending me. He's making arrangements for my food, water and ride all the way up to Yarkand."

Rasool had not told her that when he expressed his reluctance, the Wazir had replied, "You must not ask your mother and wife. They are women. You think what is best."

"Maryam's heart will be heavy if you leave so soon."

"I know, Ama. I'm very worried. Parting from you and Maryam is very difficult for me too. I have been fortunate to acquire such a good wife. This separation is almost impossible for me to bear. But unemployment is such a curse, Ama. So much money was spent on the wedding. We will need money for the winter months. Such an opportunity will not come again, Ama."

Rasool approached his bride. "I'm very disturbed, Maryam," He said in a subdued tone.

"I overheard your conversation from the garden. I will not let you go so soon," Maryam whispered in a choked voice.

"Believe me, even a moment's separation from you is unbearable for me. You know that we are poor. There are very few opportunities for employment here. With two or three trips like this, I can save enough money and start some business here."

"I have heard that this journey is very risky and life threatening. If you die, I will not be able to live." Maryam was very close to tears now.

"Death can come any time. Even within the four walls of a house." Rasool tried to console her.

Maryam sobbed softly, her arms covering her eyes.

"Believe me, if we had some money, I would not have gone. The British Joint Commissioner has asked the Wazir to send a reliable man and in the eyes of the Wazir, only *I* am reliable. This will benefit us, Maryam. Please let me go. I will try to come back soon. I will bring beautiful presents for you."

"I don't want any presents. I don't want any wealth. I just want you to be all right."

"For god's sake, let me go!" Rasool was desperate.

Maryam sobbed quietly for some more time. After a while, she said with some hesitation, "Promise me you will never go away again."

"I promise." Rasool heaved a sigh of relief.

He requested his mother on the morning of his departure, "Treat Maryam kindly, Ama. Don't taunt her or cause her any pain."

"Don't worry, Rasool," his mother reassured him. "I will treat her well. You take care of your health during the journey. Don't eat anything that will harm you. I will always pray that you don't suffer during the trip and that you return safe and healthy."

"You are such a pillar of strength, Ama. I have derived a lot of courage from your words."

He took leave from his mother and went to Maryam. Gently he told her, "Ama is a little hot tempered. Please try to get along with her."

"I will bear her temper. She will not have any reason to complain."

"You have started crying again, Maryam. Your tears make it so difficult for me."

Maryam wiped her tears. Rasool took out a five rupee note from his pocket and handed it to her. "Keep this with you. Ama does not know about this. It can be of some use to you."

She took the money silently.

"What gifts shall I bring for you?" He asked her tenderly.

"Your safe return will be the greatest gift for me," Maryam said softly.

Rasool Galwan and his companions traversed many mountains and rivers during this long journey. George Littledale, his wife, his nephew, Fletcher, and the rest of his entourage entered Tibet surreptitiously by a minor, unnamed route from Central Asia. Their destination was Lhasa, the capital of Tibet. This was kept an absolute secret because Europeans were strictly forbidden from entering Lhasa and transgressors were severely punished. For Rasool and his companions, every moment of the journey was fraught with physical hardship and dangerous experiences. As Lhasa drew closer, the number of settlements increased and it became difficult for the caravan to hide from the eyes of Tibetans. Several times, they almost came to blows with the local inhabitants. Just forty three miles from Lhasa, they were turned back forcibly by armed soldiers on horseback. They were made to take another route to Ladakh on which they encountered numerous problems in procuring food, animals and everyday necessities.

Facing these difficulties they resorted to different tactics. Rasool Galwan posed as the representative of the Dalai Lama. Kalam Rasool and Razak Akhun pretended to be monks. All three of them put on the red robes and yellow, three-cornered hats of monks. Kalam Rasool's fertile mind worked fast. He was fluent in several languages. Whenever they reached a settlement, he greeted the headman effusively, "Tashi delegs. Happiness be upon you. We are coming from Lhasa. With us is the younger sister of the British Queen, Victoria. She was the honoured guest of the Dalai Lama in Lhasa. This person here is the representative of His Holiness, the Dalai Lama. The two of us are monks. The Chinese government has sent us for the protection of the princess."

His face aglow with happiness, he would add, "We paid our respects to His Holiness and stayed in Lhasa for a month."

"Lha so, lha so, you said it right, indeed." The headman would be impressed and nod fervently in assent.

"You will be pleased to know that a friendship has been forged between England and Tibet." Kalam Rasool would continue confidently.

"Lha so, lha so, you said it right," the villagers would say.

"His Holiness has given us amulets and medicine balls.

You should keep some of this benediction for yourself." With a great show of reverence, Kalam Rasool and Razak Akhun would distribute make-believe amulets and medicine balls.

"Thugje chey." The Tibetans would thank him and innocently lift their hats and stick out their tongues to receive the blessed medicines. Once the distribution was over, the headman and the villagers would be allowed to pay their respects to the British princess reclining in the tent. Mrs Littledale assumed the role of royalty with great majesty and show.

Their secret was revealed near the border of Ladakh in Rudok, the summer capital of western Tibet. The Tibetan government fined Littledale and his party for this deception and ordered them to leave immediately. After this arduous experience, the caravan finally reached Thiksey, sixteen kilometres and a day's journey away from Leh. It was then that they decided to bake cakes to impress their wives.

The following day, they awakened early in the morning. Long hair was chopped off, beards were shaven, and old travel clothes replaced by new ones. But Razak Akhun's scheme had failed and all the cakes were charred.

"Two are only partially burnt. Shall I take them?" asked a hopeful Hussain.

"No, don't take the burnt ones. Our wives will think that these are what we ate during the journey."

Rasool gazed at Leh from a distance. He guessed the location of his house hidden in a grove. Shadows of pain flitted across his face. He prayed in his heart for the safety of his mother and wife. The last time I reached home, my wife had passed away. God forbid that my friends have kept me in the dark about some other tragedy this time. I am going home after such a long time. Please God, do not put me under any test today. Let me meet my mother and wife. If you test me after today, I will endure it.

As Leh drew nearer, Rasool's heart beat louder. He was troubled by the knowledge that Hussain and he would have to leave for Srinagar the next day with Mr and Mrs Littledale. It was November. They would have to cross the 11,578 feet high Zojila, the pass that divides the Kashmir valley from Ladakh. This was an ordeal fit only for daredevils and tempters of fate. He remembered his promise to Maryam. He had excused himself to Mr Littledale and his wife, saying that his family would not be able to bear the agony of his departure so soon after his return, but they had insisted that he go with them. "You were an asset for us on this journey," Mrs Littledale had said. "You were table boy, hunter, caravan leader, translator, clerk, doctor and tailor master. After this trip, you can spend a long time with your wife. In Leh, you must introduce us to your new bride." Rasool had not been able to refuse them.

He entered the door of his house with a heart beating fast. His face bloomed like a rose at the sight of his mother and wife in the kitchen.

"With the mercy of god and your blessings, I have returned safely," He announced to his overjoyed family.

"You took a long time for this trip. Today it has been one year, three months and thirteen days," his mother said. "Maryam and I have counted each day. After six months, we expected you to return any day. We watched for you daily but we did not receive any news about you. Poor Maryam cried so much for you."

"Ama, we travelled in barren, desert areas with no soul in sight. How could I find a man coming to Ladakh in that alien land? A few days ago, I sent a letter about my arrival with Nono Sonam Wangdus. Did you receive that?"

"Nono himself came to give the good news."

"Maryam!" Rasool remembered. "Memsaheb wants to meet you – they are returning to Kashmir tomorrow."

He persuaded Maryam to overcome her shyness and invited his mother as well. The three of them met Mr and Mrs Littledale in the Moravian Mission bungalow. Mrs Littledale greeted Maryam with a smile and asked, "How do you do?"

"Madam is asking how you are?" Rasool translated.

"I'm all right." Maryam smiled back.

"You are young and very beautiful." Rasool translated this to Ladakhi. Maryam burst out laughing. Mrs Littledale added, "Rasool will stay with you for ever after returning from Kashmir." Rasool did not translate this last sentence correctly. He wanted to spare them the misery. Mrs Littledale gave Ama and Maryam some presents and the three left happily. Outside the bungalow, Kalam Rasool and Razak Akhun were waiting with their wives to meet the saheb and memsaheb.

On reaching home, Rasool tried to explain to his mother and wife that he had to leave for Srinagar the next day.

"What are you saying, Rasool?" His mother could not hide her anguish.

"I don't wish to go but Madam and Saheb are insisting. When I have travelled for so long, what difference will another month make?"

"Do you know how much I cried thinking about you while you were gone? I would console myself with the hope of your return. Today you are talking about going again so soon after returning. If you really care about us, why would you want to go to Kashmir? We don't need so much money. Haven't you travelled enough already?"

"God knows how much I care for you all. I had refused this trip but I swear they were not ready to listen to me. They made me helpless. Madam is sick, you know."

His mother said, "We have heard there has been heavy snowfall on Zojila. Perhaps the road is blocked. How will you go?"

"I have battled such severe storms, Ama, how does a little snowfall matter? I will tear into it and return to Leh."

Rasool kept his promise that time. He returned to Leh a month later. But after spending a few months with his cherished wife, his restless feet beckoned him once again and he set off on another lengthy journey.

With the onset of summer, he accompanied an English doctor, Arthur Neve, to the Baltoro and Siachen glaciers in the Karakoram range. On returning, he opened a shop in Leh and sold tea and clothes. A few years later, he toured Central Asia and China with an American, Robert Barrett, whose recommendation and help proved valuable when he wrote his autobiography, *Servant of Sahibs*. In an editorial preface to this book, Mrs Robert Barrett quotes her husband's description of Rasool. "He is a very black, very handsome man, graceful in all of his movements, his smile most charming, his voice the sweetest man's voice I have ever heard. The woman lives not who would not fall in love at first sight but his standard of morals are very high. Women are afraid of him as a saint." In the book's Introduction, Colonel Francis Younghusband writes, "He came of the poorest. He started as a simple village lad but in every situation he behaved like a gentleman." Younghusband goes on to state, "The secret is that these men, the best of them, love adventure just as much as their employers."

Rasool was made the Aqsaqal of Leh. Aqsaqal is a Turkish word that means One-with-a-white-beard or Elder. The Aqsaqal was the local Chief Trade Officer in the transactions between Northern India and Central Asia.

Thus, Rasool acquired social status along with material possessions. But death summoned him early and on 13 March 1925, at the age of forty six, he passed away and was buried in the old graveyard of Leh. After his death, the responsibility of bringing up his two underage daughters and one son fell on the delicate shoulders of his beloved wife, Maryam.

COWARD, MADMAN, FOOL

Does he take any?"

"No."

"Commission?"

"He doesn't accept any commission."

"A gift? I mean to say, if we take it to his home …"

"I've heard that he doesn't meet any contractors at his residence."

"The coward!"

"Coward?"

"Yes, people like him appear to be something on the outside but really are something else on the inside."

"Maybe he's someone with principles."

"It's not a question of principles and all, Inder. I've bought several men like him."

"Everyone is tired of him, from the Section Officer to the Superintendent Engineer. Not a single sheet of paper returns from his room. He splits hair on every little thing."

"Can't the Superintendent make an Assistant Engineer toe the line?"

"If he wishes, he can send Murad packing."

"So the Chief must be soft on him."

"Which chief?"

"Chief Engineer Gupta Saheb. Don't you know, Ajit? He served as the Divisional Engineer here. Murad used to work under him for the Sindh Hydel Project. They say that he doesn't take any either."

"This means that there are two cowards in this place?"

"Yes."

"What will happen to my allotment then?"

"Who can say? But it's no longer a case of fifty-fifty. Barely had Murad joined the Hydel Project as Assistant Engineer when the canal near the Headworks cracked. Water leaks from the big tank. He's reported this to the Chief. Sharifuddin's payment has been stopped. David's allotment has been cancelled. It was David who had constructed the Headworks canal. The last Divisional Engineer had hiked the rate by showing that there were huge rocks to be cleared. Both of them had a blast. They used very low quality cement. It's not just their fault, Inder. Those on top also have a hand in it. Hundreds of bags of cement never arrived here."

"They say that he reported all this to the Chief a few days ago when the Chief came for a project inspection. I also heard that he complained that when the river floods, the project will be in grave danger. It looks like it will be difficult to work during his tenure. But one thing is right, yaar, he gives payments promptly, without any obstacles."

"When will the tenders for the side canal be submitted?"

"Nothing can be said yet."

"Yaar Inder, Sharifuddin hasn't given me the mithai for the last job."

"Murad has stopped his payment, so all commissions, mithais and cuts have been affected."

"We must get rid of this damned Murad."

"It won't happen as long as he has the patronage of the Chief."

"We'll get the Association to do the work for us."

"It can be done if the matter is presented in a different colour."

"How?"

"Our point will be that our project is being delayed only

because of Murad. We had aimed to complete it in a year but if Murad stays, it will require at least three to four years. This aspect should be discussed."

"Yes, it sounds appropriate," said Ajit.

"I'll raise the issue before the Association."

"But no one should get a whiff of this."

"The entire scheme will be played out with the utmost discretion," Inder assured Ajit.

Murad's home was in the Public Works Department colony. The residential quarters of the Superintendent Engineer, Jalali Saheb, the Executive Engineer, Nawang and the two Assistant Engineers, Kamran and Rajinder, were also in this colony.

Kamran was junior to Murad. His rooms had an expensive sofa set and other such furniture. Valuable rugs adorned the floors. Windows were draped with expensive curtains. He owned a colour television, a video cassette recorder, and a movie camera. Anything new in the fancy shops of Leh market made its way to Kamran's place by the following day. Now he had booked a Maruti car. Within six years of working on the project, he had built a new house and given it out on rent.

The Executive Engineer, Nawang, had one truck and two taxis that he operated in his brother's name.

Rajinder and Kamran would alternately invite Jalali Saheb to their quarters every evening. If they drank alcohol, it was nothing less than whisky, if they smoked cigarettes, they had to be Dunhills. There may have been several items which were scarce in the town, but there was no such shortage in their houses. If something was unavailable, one contractor or another arranged for it. An appetizing aroma always wafted from their kitchens, making the palate water.

Murad did not attend these parties. In the evening he often read or watched television. In his house, dal and vegetables were usually cooked for supper and he lived like one impoverished.

"Papa, Salim has a colour television." Salim was Kamran's son. "Get us one as well. Please ..." Bilal and Nadia had pleaded with him two years earlier. But despite his desire, Murad had not been able to fulfil his children's wish.

"Murad, Jamila was wearing a big gold necklace today," commented Asma one day.

Murad did not reply.

"Jamila always looks dressed up like a newly-wed bride."

Murad remained silent.

"Where does Kamran get all this money?"

"What kind of question is this, Asma?" Murad asked his wife. "You know very well."

"Yes, this is not exactly halal money." Her gloomy face belied her understanding words.

Murad believed that he could successfully combat all the temptations and avarice of this world but not face his wife's dismay or sense of deprivation. In the whole universe, only his wife could make his steps falter although he generally managed to prevail upon her on this subject. In the beginning, she would present daily reports of Kamran and Jamila's possessions, that they had this and that, that today this stuff arrived at their house. But often she would surrender to Murad's views on legitimate and illegitimate acquisitions, on morality and the day of judgement. Some of these principles were also impressed upon her own heart.

One year and two months passed since Murad had joined the Hydel Project team. Work on the project had slowed down considerably. If the original schedule was to be followed, he would have to commission the last bit of work by the following year but the possibility of this appeared very dim. The engineers had lost interest. Vegetables and dal were served in place of chicken at the parties of Jalali Saheb, Nawang, Rajinder and Kamran. Even the number of parties had decreased. Kamran and Nawang had taken to cheap cigarettes and beer in place of Dunhills and whisky. The impact was felt among the receipt clerks and peons as well. The contractors too visited the quarters less.

Then suddenly, the Chief Engineer, Gupta, was transferred. Murad found himself in hot water. Jalali Saheb was temporarily placed in charge. He removed Murad from the project and gave him small, insignificant tasks. Now, Murad reserved rooms in the Circuit House and the Government dak bungalow for VIPs and other guests and supervised the arrangements for their stay.

The project resumed its former style. The Section Officer's file went to the Assistant Engineer. From the Assistant Engineer, it reached the Executive Engineer without any hurdles. The Executive Engineer referred it to the Superintendent Engineer without editing or revision. Each person received a fixed percentage of the commission. Jalali Saheb had raised his rate, arguing that the Power Development Commissioner and the Works Minister were also paid off from his share. Murad's pending promotion was also stalled. Jalali Saheb had tampered with his confidential report.

When Murad's father heard this, he summoned Murad and scolded him. "Nono, this is the fruit of your folly. You should have compromised with circumstances."

Murad's older brother and Asma's younger brother had already labelled Murad a Fool and a Nincompoop. Asma's younger brother was a contractor and he often had heated arguments with Murad about the state of the system. They were all thieves, from top to bottom, he would rationalize. When the entire system was corrupt, then what power could a one-man crusade have? This was a matter for the mighty Government and the Public Treasury. No individual will lose anything personal and there was no burden on any one man. Murad's austerity would not make a difference in the vast ocean that was the treasury of the Government. Even if one drank a bucket of water out of it, it would not make it any less.

"The Public Exchequer is the sweat of the people," Murad would reply grimly.

"This phrase is stale and obsolete by now, Murad!" His brother-in-law would try to persuade him.

But Murad was very stubborn and obstinate. He did not listen to anyone. The transfer did not have any impact on him. Instead, he had more leisure time. But misfortune was soon to befall him. After a short illness, his daughter, Nadia, passed away. Asma was completely shattered. The tragedy was also very agonizing for Murad who, otherwise capable of enduring all kinds of difficulties, was unable to bear this loss.

"Murad, what crime did we commit that Nadia should be snatched away from us?" asked Asma, grief-stricken. "Those who commit crimes day and night do not seem to have a hair out of place."

Murad felt for a few moments that Asma was right but he hid his grief in euphemisms. "Asma, this is a severe test for us. It is God's wish. We have no choice but to accept this. Let's pray to God that we may come through this test in one piece."

The time of anguish passed. The summer brought intense heat and the waters of the river rose. In the first rush of floodwater, the dam collapsed. The back wall caved in. According to one estimate, the project received a setback of five years. Twenty five crores had been spent on the project already. This news spread like wildfire among the people. For twelve years, the people had been waiting for the completion of the project so that their dark houses could be lit by electricity. Radio, television, and government press releases had been discussing the project for over a decade and politicians had been taking credit in their speeches and statements.

The reaction of the people was extremely adverse. They organized a procession in protest. Public representatives arranged a big showdown in the Assembly. Taking Murad's name, one man said that Murad had appraised them about the misappropriation of funds earlier but his complaints had deliberately not been brought to light. Despite spending crores of rupees, the infrastructure of the dam was weak. Today, the truth was finally being revealed. Murad should be included in the Inquiry Commission.

A second member said, "During the last twelve years, many of the engineers working on the Hydel Project have built many such mini-hydel projects of their own in the form of grand houses. But where can we find the actual project itself?"

Several outraged assembly members staged a walkout.

Responding to appeals by Members, the Chief Minister handed over the matter to the Vigilance Commission. Nawang, Kamran, and Rajinder were suspended. Jalali Saheb was ordered to take a long vacation. Murad was once again given his old posting.

Before the arrival of the Vigilance Commission team, the new Chief Engineer came for an on-the-spot tour and reviewed the losses of the project. He summoned Murad to the Circuit House. "Murad, I have heard lots of favourable things about you. We need hard working, honest, and able men like you." He placed his hand on Murad's shoulder.

"Thank you, sir."

"How many years of your service remain?"

"Sixteen years, sir."

"Good. Now you have to make a lot of progress. I am convinced that the chair I occupy today will be yours in ten to twelve years."

"If your good wishes are with me, sir."

"Your promotion file is on my table. The Power Development Commissioner has sent it to me. I'll settle the case within a week or ten days."

"Thank you, sir."

"What are your views on the case connected with the Project?"

"Sir, it's a big mess, scandalous at every level. In one instance alone, seven thousand bags of cement have been embezzled."

"Murad, it is my advice that you do not involve yourself in this case. I have a feeling that there is a political hand behind this," said the Chief Engineer hesitantly.

Murad was astonished at his words.

"Sir, this is a clear case of corruption. What connection can it have with politics? A lot of people who have been hungering for electricity will be very disappointed. If the record is not straightened, it will be difficult for honest and sincere engineers to work in the future."

"Don't you worry about the future." The Chief Engineer sounded irritated. "Who has seen what comes tomorrow? Do you know how many scandals have taken place before this? The scandal of the electric wires. The diesel scandal. The machine purchase scandal. Who lost anything? The papers made a big hue and cry, splashed it in the headlines. This case will also have the same consequence. Members of the Vigilance Commission will come, complete the formalities, and then leave. But the common man will still be oppressed. In my experience, I have found this to be inevitable. Murad, listen, any negative statement from you can result in infamy for the department. Your promotion case is already in cold storage. After this, you may be transferred to some faraway place. Superior officers will be angry with you and you will be ruined."

Murad felt that it was not the Chief Engineer alone but every engineer on the project and every member of the department who was uttering these words. The Chief Engineer was quiet for a few seconds and then asked softly, "What do you intend to do?"

Murad replied with some hesitation, "Sir, if you ask me, it will be difficult for me to conceal the facts. Also the demands of duty and conscience ..."

"Arre Bhai, I'm saying this for your well-being," interrupted the Chief Engineer, "The rest is up to you and your conscience. My experience tells me that he who opposes big officers goes nowhere. Specially because the Works Minister himself is involved in the case."

"Yes, sir."

"You think about it and reply tomorrow. I have to return by the ten o'clock flight."

"Sir, I have already given you my reply," said Murad.

"Yes, but think it through again. Now you may leave." The Chief Engineer dismissed him curtly.

Bakhtiar, a big contractor associated with the Hydel Project and an intimate friend of Murad's, came to him that night. Summarizing the situation, Bakhtiar said, "Murad Bhai, at this time there are two roads in front of you. You can take the first road and present your expose before the Vigilance Commission in all its rawness, arousing the enmity of your department. Or you can choose the second road, protect your back, and get the order for your promotion. In addition, you will get a fat sum from the brotherhood of contractors. I will be personally responsible for this. But I need to have a Yes or No now."

The next morning, Bakhtiar presented his report to the Chief Engineer in the Circuit House. "Sir, he's a big fool. He spat out the morsel that was already in his mouth."

"You call him a fool," said the Chief Engineer, "That's an understatement. He is a madman of the first order."

"Coward, Madman, Fool" was published as "Buzdil, Bewaqoof, Pagal" in Ghani Sheikh's *Do Raha*, 1993.

THE LOCKED TRUNK

Today, fifty years have passed since Anwar left the trunk in Tashi's custody. Today, Tashi must end this saga. He has sent the trunk with a German tourist, lock, stock and barrel, back to its rightful owner on the other side of the border.

The tale of the trunk began with the onset of spring only a year or so before India's Independence. Roses, dahlias, sunflowers, and marigolds bloomed in the gardens of Leh. Fields abounded with white and red mustard blossoms. The fragrance of flowers filled the trees, valleys and mountains.

The British Joint Commissioner, Major Ludlow, was due to arrive in Leh. Those days, Leh was a confluence of traders from different nations. The Joint Commissioner, the highest-ranking representative of the Central Asian Ministry of Commerce, stayed in Leh for two or three months every summer. Welcome banners had been put up in Leh Bazaar to celebrate his visit. Facades of shops had been adorned with colourful frills. Officials and other such important men of Leh had journeyed to Spituk village, six kilometres away, to await his arrival. It had been thirteen days since Major Ludlow left Srinagar. The arrangements for his reception had begun with great pomp and show as soon as the news of his departure was received in Leh. Union Jacks were hoisted at every inhabited site on his route, where he was to be welcomed with great enthusiasm by the villagers.

At ten in the morning, young school children performed a march past in the Bazaar. They were dressed in khaki uniforms and red ties, with a Scouts rope around their waists and a baton balanced on their shoulders. The queue of marching children was long. Tashi stood near the end of the line. Anwar stood in front of him. They were both students in the second standard.

The children marched with their red batons to the seventeenth century mosque, the Jamma Masjid, where a crowd of spectators had gathered. A band headed the parade. There were other performers as well, most of them women. The crowd watched the little marchers affectionately. Tashi spotted his father in the crowd. He preened, chest expanding with pride, convinced that in the heart of every marching child there must swell just such a sense of superiority.

"Halt!" The voice of the Drill Master, Ghulam Sultan, rang out, and the band stopped. Master Sultan was famous for his agility and vigour. He put the metal microphone close to his mouth.

"Ladies and Gentlemen," Master Sultan broadcast the news in a loud voice. "British Joint Commissioner, Major Ludlow Saheb, is arriving in Leh today. You must also join the children in extending a heartfelt welcome to him."

The bandmaster issued a command and the band resumed playing.

"Right turn! March!" The children marched forward and stood in two rows near the gate of the Bazaar.

"Sit down!" The children sat down. A few women waited behind them, dressed in fine clothes, white silken scarves on their hats, holding buckets of milk and buttermilk and pitchers of alcohol, as was customary for greeting honoured guests. In the afternoon, a platoon of the Dogra army arrived from Leh Fort. These smart, young, armed soldiers queued in front of the children.

The children had been very alert in the morning but by the afternoon they had lost much of their enthusiasm. Gradually, they began to sneak away.

"Balti, where are you going?" Master Sultan demanded.

"Sir, I'm really thirsty," Anwar replied.

"Did you ask anyone?"

Anwar did not answer.

"Balti, do you know what this is?" Master Sultan raised his stick. Anwar maintained his silence.

"They call this Force and Power. Return to your place!" Chastised, Anwar returned to his seat. He was a resident of Baltistan. His father was a clerk of the Wazir, and it was because of this connection that he was nicknamed Balti.

The Headmaster repeatedly took out his pocket watch to look at the time. Suddenly, the school watchman, completely out of breath, came running towards him. He began saying something to the Headmaster and Master Sultan. Master Sultan jumped toward the children and blew his whistle loud and long. The children sprung to attention and stood upright with their batons. A few minutes later, the procession of the Joint Commissioner reached the gate of the Bazaar. His peons and staff members were leading the way. The peons had on uniforms of a thick, red fabric. Beautiful turbans with colourful fringes rested on their heads. Sashes, with the crest of King George the Fifth embroidered in the centre, adorned their waists. Their gait spoke of tremendous importance and firmness.

Major Ludlow got down from his horse, glorious in his riding pants, long boots, and imposing hat. Officials and dignitaries followed him, flanked by graceful, neighing horses with sweeping tails, smart gaits, and raised ears, decorated in priceless trappings of splendour. The status associated with cars these days was displayed through horses in those times.

In the eyes of Tashi and the other children, the Joint Commissioner was an extraordinary personality, to be stared at with fear and respect. The soldiers presented the Guard of Honour and the Joint Commissioner moved towards the crowd. The band saluted him. Then it was the children's turn to perform the Guard of Honour with their batons. Major Ludlow took off his hat to acknowledge the salute. Two children presented him with bouquets.

Master Sultan's voice boomed in all directions. "Three Cheers for the Joint Commissioner, Major Ludlow Saheb Bahadur. Hip, Hip …"

"Hurrah!" The children cheered loudly.

"Hip, hip …"

"Hurrah!"

The crowd parted as the Joint Commissioner passed through. Following him were the king, Dadul Namgyal, the wazir of Ladakh, Lala Amarnath, the tehsildar, Thakur Surdev Singh, the nayab tehsildar, Raja Ashraf Khan and other officials of Leh. The procession stopped at Karzoo Garden by the Joint Commissioner's bungalow. This garden was named after Viceroy Lord Curzon but Ladakhis called it Karzoo Garden. A Union Jack flapped on a tallish edifice that loomed over this grand area. When the children reached the garden, the Joint Commissioner was seated on a fancy chair on a raised platform. Officials and dignitaries were seated on chairs to his left and right. The children gathered to one side of the green lawn. Then Anwar and two other boys sang "God Bless Our Gracious King!" for the long life and prosperity of King George the Fifth. The seated spectators all stood up to show respect. The Joint Commissioner gave the children a gift and the ceremony ended.

Two days later, the Joint Commissioner's visit was the main topic of conversation at Tashi's school. Usually, during the fourth hour of the school day, classes were broken up into three groups. One group studied Arabic with the Maulvi, the second studied Hindi with Guruji, and the third was tutored in Bodhi by Geshe Yeshes Tundup. But that day, classes were not divided in this manner. Instead, Maulvi Saheb and Guruji dragged their chairs next to each other. The students were happy to have free time but the high, passionate voice of Maulvi Saheb startled them. Their attention shifted towards him.

"Lamaji, why are you sitting so far away? Come here!" Maulvi Saheb said to Geshe Yeshes Thundup. "Lamaji, this white Commissioner is a guest for a few days now and very soon, he'll pack his bags to cross the ocean and leave Hindustan."

Guruji agreed, "He will definitely go. Now India is to have self rule."

"Self rule! Independence! Such ideas are not possible for us. Just yesterday, all the people were lowering their eyes in front of the Joint Commissioner so why will this white man leave?"

"Mark my words, this white Britisher will be the last officer of Ladakh," said the Maulvi to the Geshe. "Yesterday I heard on the radio ..."

Radio? The children perked up. Those days, only two or three people had a radiogram. Among them was Norman Driver, a missionary priest. His radiogram was powered by a big turbine and a twelve volt battery. Another radio was energized by a big wheel in the compound of a Kashmiri doctor's residence. Tashi and his friends took great pleasure in turning this wooden wheel. Anwar, Tashi, Sonam and a few others would collect in the veranda daily where eight or ten men gathered to listen to the radio. Among them were also three or four Ladakhis who held strong political views. Speeches of the leaders of Pakistan and Hindustan were broadcast on the radio. "This is Mahatma Gandhi." "This is Mohammad Ali Jinnah." "This is Pandit Jawaharlal Nehru." "This is Liaqat Ali Khan." For those who did not understand the language, the gist of the speeches were translated and explained. A heated discussion always followed. Tashi and Anwar couldn't even understand Urdu. The changing facial expressions, the raised voices, the interests and arguments of the elders hearing these speeches, were a constant puzzle to them.

Maulvi Saheb was talking about independence but the children were not interested in these things. They were focussed on the colourful spectacle of the much-anticipated cultural show that was to take place the day after in honour of the Joint Commissioner.

And so, in this manner, the year passed. When and how freedom came, they did not even know. On the day of Independence, there were no celebrations. No patriotic songs were played and no slogans shouted in the town of Leh. The country was partitioned into Hindustan and Pakistan. A hazy feeling descended upon the region.

The English Joint Commissioner had left Ladakh a month earlier. Lala Amarnath had gone off with his delegation to the winter capital of Skardo. Skardo was in Baltistan, a region incorporated into Ladakh by the Dogra administration. The

Wazir spent six months of the winter in Skardo and six months of the summer in Leh. Anwar's father had also left with the Wazir but because of his annual exams, Anwar had stayed behind with an uncle who had a shop in Leh in which he sold apricots, butter and grains. In October 1947, Kashmir was attacked by rebel forces but the faint rumours of strife were confirmed in Ladakh only when the army of the Maharaja revolted and joined the Gilgit Scouts to surround Skardo. Then the news flew in that Lala Amarnath had been assassinated in Skardo.

One day, in the early hours of the morning, Anwar came to Tashi's house, lugging a big trunk behind him.

"Azhang Tundup, I am going to Skardo with my uncle, Mustafa," he said to Tashi's father. "You keep this trunk with you. Please send it if you find someone going to Skardo."

Tashi's heart sank. "Don't go to Skardo, Anwar. Stay in Leh."

"The situation in Skardo is bad these days," his father agreed. "You must have heard." Anwar nodded his head.

"There is fighting in Skardo. Don't go, Anwar," Tashi pleaded with him.

"Azhang Mustafa is going. I have to accompany him."

"Let him go. You stay with us."

"When I return next year, the situation will have returned to normal."

"How can Anwar stay?" Tashi's father tried to reason with Tashi. "His parents and relatives are in Skardo, his house is there."

Anwar got up to leave and Tashi's father patted his head affectionately. He pulled out his wallet and gave him a rupee.

Then Anwar shook Tashi's hand. As he was leaving, he reminded Tashi's father about the trunk again. "If you don't find anyone, then next year when Aba comes to Leh he will take it himself."

"Wa, this is your property. If I find a good man, I will send it with him. Or else I will definitely send it next year."

But Anwar never returned the next year or ever after.

Two months after his departure, invading Kabila forces from the west gradually advanced towards Leh. Sounds of exploding cannon balls and gunfire echoed in the town. People were panic-stricken. Until then, Buddhists and Muslims had lived like brothers. Now they had an unwritten agreement amongst themselves that they would aid each other in times of danger.

During those days, a new army officer, Colonel Parab, was the head of the armed forces and civilians in Leh. The civil bureaucracy was dead so the Colonel set up a Cabinet. He appointed a Buddhist, Kalon Rigzin, as Minister of Defence, a local Muslim, Khwaja Abdullah Shah, as Home Minister, a Christian, Eliezer Joldan, as Education Minister and Mary Driver, the wife of an English missionary who ran a hospital in Leh, as Health Minister. To head them all, Norman Driver, the missionary, was made Prime Minister. The Cabinet had no special work.

In November, the attacking Kabila army was defeated. For several years, there was no news of Anwar. Tashi and his friends made wish-horses fly for news of Anwar and his parents. But it was as if a Berlin Wall had been raised between Baltistan and Ladakh. No information was forthcoming. The steel trunk was kept carefully in Tashi's room. He did not permit anyone to touch it. As the years went by, the large, heavy trunk Anwar had staggered in with slowly grew smaller and smaller in size.

When the Nehru-Liaqat pact was signed and communication lines opened up, Tashi wrote a letter to Anwar, referring to the trunk and asking how he should send it since there was no one coming or going and no other option was in sight. Anwar's reply was enthusiastic. He wrote to say that he did remember his childhood companion. About himself, he wrote that he had passed his matriculation exams. He did not mention the trunk in his letter.

Rarely did any person visit Leh from Baltistan during that period. From Ladakh also, only a few men crossed the border and then too, their destination was Lahore or Islamabad. In 1970, a Mr Jaffer arrived in Ladakh from Baltistan. The man had familial roots in Ladakh but had settled in Skardo and obtained a high post there even before the Partition. Meanwhile, Tashi had joined the Ladakh Scouts and was to be shortly stationed at the Siachen glacier to defend the frontiers against Pakistan. Hearing of Mr Jaffer's arrival, he entreated him to carry Anwar's trunk to Baltistan. Mr Jaffer informed him that Anwar Hussain was a teacher and lived with his family in the village of Ganok. No roads linked that area with the rest of the country. It would be very difficult to transport anything there.

"Send it by mail. I'll pay." Tashi insisted.

"Don't embarrass me like that, Nono. Of course, I'll carry a few things with me," Mr Jaffer tried to compromise but Tashi decided to wait. He didn't know which items would be relevant to Anwar and he was sure that there would be other travellers to Baltistan. But the war with Pakistan followed soon after and Ladakh changed rapidly. Roads, tourists and technology altered it drastically.

Tashi joined the Indian Army and gradually rose in rank. One by one, he watched his comrades sacrifice their lives in the icy Siachen, that distant, disputed battlefield on the Karakoram range where Indian and Pakistani troops risk death every day. Tashi's heart froze like glacial ice whenever Baltistan was mentioned.

One day, his father summoned him to his bedside and said, "Tashi, I am worried about you. You have scaled the highest peaks and acquired all these medals and badges. You are brave and strong. Yet instead of walking, you march around the house. You speak as if you are commanding a unit of soldiers. My life is almost over now. It is you who will have to keep the family together. Not just with discipline but with gentleness as well."

A few days later, he passed away. With this tragedy, the trunk that lay in the corner of his room became more and more repugnant to Tashi. It seemed to spread like cancer and occupy all the air in that space. Occasionally, some acquaintances headed for Baltistan offered to carry a few things with them. But Tashi was adamant. He refused to break open the lock of the trunk. Anwar would receive it as he had left it. He would know that people on the other side had integrity too and were not interested in looting his possessions. Unable to open the trunk, Tashi vacated the room where it was stored, placed a huge padlock on the door, and hid the key.

And now, fifty years after the day Anwar left, he was finally able to rid himself of the trunk. A German tourist, Peter

Hoffman, who was staying in his guesthouse, had agreed to take it. Moved by Tashi's story, Hoffman said, "It is in my itinerary to visit Skardo, Shigar and Khapulu. Now I will travel to Ganok as well and meet Anwar Hussain in person and give him these things."

Tashi hoped to feel a deep sense of relief when the trunk was gone. He opened the doors to the room again. But a strange disquiet lingered in his heart.

Just a few days after Peter Hoffman had left, a letter arrived from Baltistan. In it, Anwar had notified him of the death of his parents. "I never wanted my trunk back, Tashi Namgyal," he had written. "I thought if you had it, it would act as a bond between us. I always kept the hope alive that I would return. But now I am requesting you to send it. I apologize for the inconvenience. In the trunk, there are things that belonged to Ama and Aba – a teapot and a shirt that will remain mementoes for the beautiful time I spent with them in Leh. I would like you to keep the cups as a remembrance of our childhood."

Tashi could not control the flood of sadness and elation that swept over him. He wanted to reply, "Anwar Hussain, I would have sent your trunk earlier but I did not find anyone to send it with. That is not quite true. At first, I did not let Aba look for anyone because having your trunk comforted me and gave me hope that you would come back. After that, you know how the relations between our nations changed. I did not want to open the lock. I didn't want to be the target of Pakistani suspicions. I was afraid of the memories that lurked in the trunk. Now your letter has set me free."

Instead, he wrote at the first opportunity, informing Anwar that he had sent his trunk with a reliable man and expressing deep regrets for the death of his parents. He ended the letter with a promise. "Nowadays, beautiful copper teapots are made in Leh, engraved with intricate silver panels. Next time I will send you one, my friend."

Two and a half months later, Tashi received a letter from Frankfurt.

Dear Mr Namgyal,

On reaching Baltistan, I went to Ganok straightaway where I had no trouble finding Anwar Hussain's house. But he is not in this world anymore. He passed away one month ago. His house was locked. I found out that his wife had left for her parents' village. I was forced to open the trunk at the airport for a Customs' inspection. In it, I found books and papers, a shirt and a teapot, some utensils and two cups for daily use. The shirt is useless; its collar is torn. Time and termites have done their work. The teapot is worn and its colour has faded. At the bottom of the trunk, I discovered a child's baton wrapped with a red tie. Shall I send all these things to you?

THE SMILE

The jeep passed by like a fragrant puff of the morning breeze and left Sonam clutching his restless heart. In this jeep sat Angmo and her companions. Unwittingly, a hope surfaced in Sonam's heart that at the next bend, the jeep would meet with such a pleasant accident that Angmo's exquisite body would not receive even a single scratch. That he would run up to the wrecked jeep, collect Angmo in his arms, and carry her to the army hospital nearby where she would look at him with gratitude through her half-open eyes. But the jeep survived the dangerous mountain bend and raced onto the straight road, disrupting the sequence of his reverie.

On both sides of the road, men and women, young and old, in splendid new clothes, were walking towards the Spituk monastery for the annual Gustor festival held during the eleventh month of the Buddhist calendar. He saw the jeep turn to the right of the mountain and disappear from sight. A thought struck him like a bolt of lightning. Holding on to the wall of a graveyard, he climbed the mountain hastily. Within minutes, he reached the summit. The jeep emerged on the crooked road that curved between the rocky lands spread as far as the eye could see. In the far distance, triangular peaks, cloaked in snow and bathed by the cool rays of the morning sun, conversed with the sky. After driving on the tarmac road which was under repair, the jeep moved to a sandy stretch, leaving clouds of dust in its trail. Wavering and meandering on the bumpy dirt track, it once again reached the tarmac road. Now the jeep was within view, moving towards the rocks to Tongray Zampa where a wooden ford had been built above a stream, on the edge of which was written, "Large vehicles are prohibited on this bridge."

The worn-out signboard and its faded letters danced before Sonam's eyes. For a few moments, the same sinister hope re-entered his mind that the jeep would meet with an accident at the centre of the bridge and flying like a bird, he would whisk Angmo away to safety. But as though it were mocking this desire of his, the jeep crossed the bridge safely and raced onto the even road ahead. It disappeared as it descended, only to reappear as a tiny, black speck that gradually receded into a black spot before his eyes. Sonam began thinking that Angmo was in that black dot. All his happiness and hopes were contained in that speck. If only he could get Angmo, he could experience paradise in this life. A sensation of thrilled anticipation overcame him.

The moving black speck was momentarily concealed from his hungry eyes. He cast a glance downward from the Kigu Brag mountain. Several people were heading towards the festival on foot as they did not have any vehicle. Once again, Sonam looked up and his sweeping gaze took in the range, from the peaks to the foothills of the mountains. As he sped downward, loosened pebbles clattered as they fell. He stopped by a small boulder for a few moments to regain balance and in the next instant, was lost in the crowd on the road.

Sonam reached Spituk monastery an hour and a half later. Thousands of spectators were enjoying the mask dance from rooftops, balconies, windows, walls, and open courtyards. Beautiful bejewelled women from noble households were watching the courtyard from windows decorated with painted carvings. Sonam's probing eyes searched all four directions. His gaze encountered the colourful Buddha, decked in embroidered silks, and came to pause before the ornate windows. Angmo was leaning against a pillar near a window, surrounded by her friends. Pushing his way through the crowd, Sonam positioned himself so he could see her clearly. Sometimes, when he saw the eyes of the spectators who sat on the rooftops and courtyards fall on the balconies and windows, he felt all those eyes were on Angmo. In this crowd, he did not feel hesitant or nervous staring at Angmo continuously. When the person standing next to him drew his attention to the riveting mask performance in the courtyard before them, Sonam was embarrassed and glared at the man. How does he know why I came here, he muttered to himself.

After some time, people began dispersing for the afternoon meal. Angmo and her friends also rose from the window. Jostling and shoving through the throng, Sonam entered the courtyard that looked like a sea of people rising in waves. He walked down the new stone steps where, at every turn, makeshift shops perched on small plots of land. Through the tent coverings of some of these shops, he could see pakoras and samosas being fried and Lipton tea being brewed. He requested a cup of tea and taking out dry rotis from his bag, dipped them in the tea and began eating. He finished his cup and ordered another as he still had one roti left. After eating, he made his way back to the rooftop. By then Angmo and her friends had also returned.

A little while later, Sonam saw Angmo get up from her place and disappear from the window. He raced through the crowds to the back of the monastery and stood near the door. Women gleamed with jewels as they came and went but Angmo was not among them. He could see some men sipping alcohol under a chorten. Beyond them, a scratchy, lazy dog peed, lifting his leg onto a stone. Despondent, Sonam climbed to the roof again. Angmo had returned to the window. Leaning against the edge of the window to watch her, he felt the earlier exhilaration return.

It was only a few days ago that he had been introduced to Angmo, although, for a long time, he had known of her as one of the most beautiful women in town. Sonam's melodious voice was very popular. One of Angmo's friends had requested him to sing a song. All said and done, although he did not possess any wealth, degree or position, this mellifluous voice was his only asset and he spent it liberally. Smiling a lethal smile, Angmo had praised his singing.

For a few moments, Angmo's smile bloomed in front of Sonam like a beautiful flower. During the last eight to ten days, that flowery smile had blossomed in front of his eyes several times. And each time, he had felt a pang of intoxicated pleasure.

The sun was setting slowly, moving from the top of the tall monastery towards the triangular snow-covered peak in the west. The number of spectators was decreasing every moment. Windows, balconies, and edges of rooftops were emptying out. Sonam waited for Angmo to leave.

When Angmo and her friends rose, Sonam got up as well. As the crowd had thinned, he was able to reach the back door quickly. One or two persons were coming through the door. Two men were arguing. Sonam deliberately untied the lace of his left boot. He rehearsed once more the beautiful words with which he would address Angmo.

Sonam waited with anxiety and impatience. Suddenly, Angmo appeared with her friends, her beauty blossoming, flowering, raising a hundred riots with every step. A tremor ran through Sonam's body. He hastily began to tie his shoe laces.

As she passed by, he summoned some courage and asked, "Angmo-ley, how did you like the fair?"

"Excuse me?" Angmo's voice lacked recognition. She moved on, gripping her friend's arm.

Sonam stared into the darkness spreading before his eyes and realized that the flowering smile had withered.

"The Smile" was published as "Muskurahat"in *Hamara Adab* in 1970. It was translated into Hindi by Savera Ahmed. This translation was reproduced for the literary section of *Punjab Kesari* in January 1982.

HOPES AND DESIRES

The fifteenth and sixteenth days of the first Buddhist month bring happy tidings every year. On these days, devotees celebrate the conception of Buddha Sakyamuni and pray that their wishes be fulfilled. They are special times when new families are formed and new relationships forged.

Kunzes waited with bated breath for these days to arrive. For a long time, a hope had kindled in her heart that she would be blessed with a brother. Her eyes opened early on the morning of the fifteenth day. She put on her clothes, folded the bedding, and started on her daily chores. She carried her pot to fetch water from the stream. Her mother lit the stove while she was gone. On coming home, Kunzes swept the area between her room and the main door and cleaned the bowls and plates displayed on the wooden shelves. This was her contribution to the daily tasks at home and it could not be allotted to anyone else.

She went about her chores hastily so that she could leave for the pilgrimage around the holy shrines of Leh, all within a mile of her home. Due to the impending trip, she could not go to collect cowdung and did not venture to any other house in the community to offer her services. The three goats belonging to her family were entrusted to a neighbour's son to be grazed with the rest of the flock at Abhi Tshas.

Freed from her work at last, she reached the market, carrying with her a bag of boiled peas. Her friends, waiting on the steps of a shop, had brought some yos or roasted barley grain. The three friends purchased half a kilo of mustard oil to light the butter lamps at the feet of the Buddha and walked toward Sankar monastery.

Men and women of all ages were heading for Sankar. There

were hordes of children at every corner along the way. With their shirts spread in front of them, the children were chanting, Ali re, bali re, khab re, khabchag re, rumbu re, rumchag re, jaoo re, jabtse re – Give us an earring, give us ear hoops, give us a needle, even a broken one, give us a shell, even a broken shell, give us a coin, give us tweezers … But neither a needle nor a shell, nor crisp notes or coins were tossed into the laps of the young plaintiffs. All the pilgrims did, however, offer some boiled peas and roasted grain. Kunzes also placed her hand in her bag and took out some boiled peas which she handed to the children. There were eight or ten children in the first group itself and very soon her bag was reduced to half its size.

Then a second group appeared and then a third. Kunzes and her friends moved ahead, a few grains of yos and peas in their hands to offer the children. There were several groups of children near Sankar monastery too. They too had converted their outstretched clothes into begging bowls and were chanting the Ali re, bali re refrain and other sacred mantras. When Kunzes walked ahead without giving them anything, they wrapped themselves around her legs and it was only after she had tossed them a couple of peas each that she managed to release herself from their clutches.

Numerous devotees, including some nuns, were sitting at the door of Sankar monastery. Their eyes were half-open and their lips chapped from hunger and cold. Some of the men had draped woollen shawls around their shoulders. All of them were silently uttering mantras, rotating the beads of their rosaries between two fingers. These devotees were observing a ritual fast which required them to refrain from speaking. Kunzes paused before them and praised them in her heart. Then she quietly followed her friends and entered the monastery.

People were kowtowing before the statue of Chenrezig, the Buddha of Compassion, and other deities. Butter lamps were burning before these images. Kunzes and her friends poured oil in many of the lamps, kowtowed before the statues, and circumambulated them, calling for blessings to fulfil their youthful hopes and desires.

Several desires dwelled in the depths of Kunzes's heart. Ripe in her heart was the hope of meeting her lover who had vanished from her eyes after stirring so many dreams in the temple of her mind. She yearned to see her ailing mother get well again. Moreover, a desire had settled deep within her that on the following day, during the chos-spun rituals, where kinship was created through religious sanction, she would be fortunate enough to acquire a nice brother. Among her wishes, there lingered this fantasy too, that she would possess a five or six lined perag. She craved for this head adornment for married Buddhist women made by sewing pieces of turquoise and coral onto a strip of leather. She knew that a perag with several lines of precious stones was a sign of affluence. Kunzes had collected a hundred and twenty five rupees by hoarding the pennies she had earned selling grass and dung. In these times, however, when turquoise was so expensive, they seemed too insignificant for an entire perag. Kunzes did not expect this old desire of hers to be fulfilled.

Dolma, who lived in a house adjacent to Kunzes's, had obtained a seven-lined perag in just one year. Her friend, Dolkar, had a huge nine-lined perag. The thought crossed Kunzes's mind that Dolkar's husband was wealthy and that she had inherited a five-lined perag from her mother that she had later increased into a nine-lined one.

Kunzes reiterated these wishes in her mind several times as she knelt before the statues. Mother, lover, perag, and chosspun brother – all merged together and soared in her consciousness.

When she came out with her friends, other pilgrims had entered the gates of the monastery and many others were moving toward the Namgyal Tsemo. A long line of people was inching its way toward the temple. At regular intervals, groups of children were crying in high voices, Ali re, bali re. Kunzes's bag was empty. Embarrassed, she walked past the children quickly.

The path to the summit was very narrow and there were thick piles of snow on both sides. An old woman stood resting in one spot, rotating rosary beads, staring up at her destination. Sometimes, the path seemed to reach a dead end but together with her spry friends, Kunzes squeezed her way from left or right and moved ahead. When the three of them reached the summit, the sun was shining directly overhead and the monastery, approximately five hundred years old, was bathed in the glow of gleaming sunlight.

Despite many hardships, devotees were making the circular ascent from the foot of the mountain with profound faith. Prostrating themselves on the ground, they would rise in unison, recite mantras for the happiness of all sentient beings, fold both hands, raise them above their heads, and lie prone again. Extending their hands in front of them, they would carve arcs on the earth with pointed horns and objects and then rise once more. They repeated this motion with every step. The procession looked very picturesque from above. Kunzes and her friends watched their movements for a long time and then the three of them entered the Red Temple with its huge three-storeyed image of Chamba, the Buddha of the Future.

First, they poured oil in the lamps and pressed their foreheads to the statue. People had stuck coins and needles on the walls of the temple. Kunzes's friends offered a two anna coin each and she donated a red one paisa coin with a hole in its centre. Next, they visited the adjoining Tsemo Gonkhang temple where there was a statue of the guardian deity, Mahakala.

Coming out of the temple, the three friends descended from the Tsemo. Along the path several children were chanting, Ali re, bali re. They had boiled peas and grains of roasted barley in their laps and were eating as they sang. God knows when and where this sequence of children will break, Kunzes thought. In resignation, she showed the children her empty bag even as her friends took out the yos from their big bags and handed them over.

The three friends reached the magnificent Leh palace built by the famous king, Singge Namgyal, who ruled Ladakh from 1616-1642. At one time, this palace teemed with inhabitants and there was much hustle-bustle in its vicinity but its importance as the main royal residence declined when the royal Namgyal family moved to the village of Stok after the Dogra forces conquered Ladakh in the mid-nineteenth century. Kunzes gazed downward from the edge of the temple near the palace. Only rooftops were visible below. People could be seen on them, viewing the palace above. Bundles of grass were lined up on some rooftops while some had dung cakes and small sticks of wood spread out to dry. Skipping, jumping, searching, Kunzes's eyes found the small rooftop of her house and stopped. With its modest twigs of willow and tiny piles of cow dung stacked in one corner, it appeared just like the top of a table in a big office. Oh, only this much dung remains with us, she thought. How expensive wood and dung have become this year! Perhaps the pile looks small from afar, she tried to console herself. Her gaze slipped from the rooftop and fell upon the black speck on the clothesline in the garden. She felt waves of shame engulf her. The black speck was her shirt, torn in several places. She had worn this shirt under her long robe continuously for the last two years. Only this morning had she changed into a shirt of red flannel. Her gaze dropped to her collar. The sight of the bright, new redness of her outfit stirred a ripple of deep pleasure in her subconscious, expressing itself as a mysterious smile on her lips. Then suddenly, she remembered the old, dirty shirt and bashful again, stared at it fixedly. But then she smiled once more. How foolish I am. I have such far reaching thoughts. After all, who can see that shirt of mine at this time?

Kunzes's friends, Nyima and Padma, were watching the dwarf-like people below. Seeing Kunzes rapt in thought, Nyima nudged her with her elbow. "Hey you, who are you thinking of?"

"No one." Kunzes was embarrassed.

"Then what are you staring at so wide eyed?"

"I was thinking something."

"What were you thinking? Tell us as well," said the mischievous Padma, playing with Kunzes's braided hair.

"Why should I tell you?" Kunzes turned her face away enigmatically and the three of them burst out laughing.

One after another, they visited all the shrines in the vicinity.

Then, just as the sun was about to set, the three of them descended from the mountain. Now the only temple left to visit was the Jokhang Temple in the New Monastery complex. The temple stood in the middle of Leh town, on the old site of the District Commissioner's office. It housed a copper statue of Jo Rimpochey brought all the way from Tibet. Built to provide a common place of worship for different Buddhist sects, the temple had been consecrated in 1962, on the occasion of Buddha Jayanti.

The three friends entered this temple and saw with their own eyes the lamp that consumed a maund of oil and blazed for an entire year. Kunzes and her friends had run out of oil. Nyima and Padma offered some one paisa coins but Kunzes didn't even have a single penny. Taking off her hat, she pulled out a needle, and offered just that. For the last time, Kunzes repeated her wishes and hopes in front of the image of Jo Rimpochey. She felt as though a big burden had been lifted from her heart. For the last time, she wiped the dust from her forehead. The three friends straightened their clothes and moved towards their houses.

Kunzes's heart was thumping as she entered her house. She had taken so much time. Her mother would reprimand her for this delay and grumble at her as usual. She crept to her room nervously. Her mother was sitting beside the stove, head slumped, groaning from the pain of her chronic illness. The room was filled with smoke. She did not hear Kunzes come in. Kunzes lifted a clay pot quietly and went to fetch water.

The sixteenth day dawned. On this day too, several visitors were headed for Sankar monastery where amulets were being distributed and where the annual chos-spun ceremony was to be held. Those persons who wanted to enter the chos-spun community had to send a delicate trinket marked with their names. Some sent rings while others submitted bracelets, some presented clips to grip the hair and others bunches of keys. On the sixteenth day of the first month, a monk would mix all these objects in a huge vessel and pair them together. In the evening, the paired objects would be divided among their owners. If the owner of one object happened to be male and the other female, then a brother-sister relationship would be established between the two. The relationship between a young girl and elderly woman would be that of mother and daughter. If, in the end, one sole object remained, it would either be merged with an existing pair or the owner would be coupled with some deity.

Kunzes wished that she would be linked with a young man who she could claim as her brother because she did not have one of her own. She set out for Sankar monastery in the morning with her friend, Angmo, taking with her an old, worn-out brass ring that she marked with a green thread. She also took a fake piece of coral that belonged to her friend, Padma. Angmo took a silver ring. Handing over these things to a monk, Angmo and Kunzes made offerings with profound respect and received amulets from the high monk. Kunzes tied the knotted thread he gave her to her button and Angmo placed hers around her neck.

The hours passed by very slowly for Kunzes. She performed the household tasks mechanically. Her mind was fixed upon the brass ring with the green thread strung through it. Who knows what is in my fate – a brother, sister, mother or father!

Who knows, I may be paired with the goddess, Dolma. Grace and bounty will then be showered upon my house.

Her mother also had a chos-spun brother whom she was very close to. In the twenty six years that had passed since their relationship was formed, the world had changed many colours. Several revolutions had occurred in their town but that did not make an iota of difference to their love. Kunzes's elder sister, who was now married, had a Muslim brother. Kunzes remembered that day clearly when the Muslim brother had placed a scarf of white silk around her sister's neck and rising in joy, her sister had greeted him amidst the clanging of her white conch bracelets. From that time onward, they invited each other during the festivals of Id and Losar. And Rashid had become not just her sister's but also like her own big brother.

By the time Kunzes finished her work, the day was nearly over. She set off for the courtyard of the monastery. Already, a crowd had assembled there. She waited impatiently for the distribution of paired objects. After a while, the distribution began. Kunzes shoved her way into the crowd.

The presiding monk was holding up pairs of objects in his hand and asking, "Whose things are these?"

"That's mine." A hand was extended.

"And the other mine." A second hand reached out and the two kindred came together.

"And this?" The monk held up another pair.

"The silver chain is mine," said a female voice.

"And the golden hook mine," responded a male one. Brother and sister, newly united, greeted each other.

After some time, the fake coral of her friend, Padma, was

held up. A key was joined to it. "Whose key and coral are these?"

A girl claimed the key but as Padma was absent, Kunzes shouted from the crowd, "The coral belongs to Padma, my friend." She stretched out her hand and took the coral. A fair-skinned girl, approximately the same age as her, approached her and introduced herself as Salma. The girl asked Kunzes for the coral and sent a message of sisterhood to Padma.

Brother and sister, brother and brother, father and son were embracing each other. There was much love in the air. Kunzes's heart was thumping in hopeful anticipation.

The items exhibited next were a thin bracelet of iron and a small piece of blue turquoise.

"Whose are these?" The monk dangled the two objects and surveyed the crowd.

"The turquoise is mine," answered a female voice.

"The iron bracelet is mine," replied a young man, popping his head out. It was Tshering, the blacksmith. Leaping hastily, he reached out for the bracelet but the mistress of the blue turquoise did not come forward.

"This blue turquoise?" The monk's booming voice echoed but no one came forward to claim it.

A resounding silence descended on the gathering. Tshering, the blacksmith's face turned a deeper shade of black and he stared longingly and silently at the piece of blue turquoise. Kunzes understood that the turquoise girl had probably not come forward for fear that a relation with a lower caste person would disgrace her. Tshering's caste was low because he worked as a smith. His hands were often black as he was in constant contact with pots, pans and coal.

Just a few moments ago, Kunzes had been experiencing a strange euphoria but now she was disheartened. The paired items were being exhibited one by one but her eyes were frozen on Tshering's face. He was desperately kneading the piece of turquoise in his hands which he had obtained by claiming that he would enquire about its owner himself. Kunzes felt that Tshering's eyes were brimming with tears and his heart was shattered. An anguished pang arose in her heart.

As she watched the distribution process in disillusionment, her worn brass ring appeared, joined with a beautiful, gold ring. A handsome young man claimed the gold ring.

"And whose ring is this?" The monk asked for the second time, displaying it in all four directions.

Kunzes was about to walk up but her steps halted. She felt as if her tongue had been tied down. Quietly, she left the crowd and approached Tshering who was standing alone at a distance, observing, with restless eyes, people in the crowd shake hands with one another.

"Is the piece of turquoise with you?" she asked.

"Yes, it is."

"That's mine."

"It's yours?" Tshering's sad face brightened at once.

"Yes." Kunzes looked at him and smiled. "You are my brother from today."

She saw teardrops shimmering like pearls in Tshering's eyes. She hoped they were tears of happiness.

"Hopes and Desires" was published as "Arzuen" in *Pamposh* in July 1958.

A FORSAKEN PARADISE

Father: I reached the spot where I had first confessed my love to my beloved. I could barely recognize the place. Concrete houses and government offices stretched as far as the eye could see. I wondered whether I was dreaming. Forty years had passed. Could these be the same badlands where wild animals roamed free all day long? Could this be the same abode of ghosts and spirits people feared to tread after dusk?

For a few minutes, I thought this was not the place I had been looking for. If it hadn't been for the three hundred and seventy five year old palace looming on the mountain before me, my doubt would have turned to certainty.

I stepped off the concrete road onto the little path meandering between the houses and disappeared at the edge of the mountain. Two cars passed by, raking up clouds of dust. I came upon an official signboard with "Ministry of Desert Development" written on it. Frantically I began searching for the little rock in front of the chorten on which Angmo and I had promised to stay together for eternity. That was the day of the Shey srub-lha, the harvest festival celebrated in the ancient capital of Shey on the banks of the river Indus. Angmo had slipped away from the festival to meet me here.

"For you," she had said, "I will reject all the wealth and riches of the world."

In reply I had answered, "I will fill your world with happiness."

Angmo had talked and I had listened. Then I had talked and she had listened. How time passed, I cannot say for sure.

"Look, Phuntsog," Angmo had cried out seeing two mountain birds fly together over us, "How fortunate they are." A rabbit that emerged from a mountain hole had hesitated for a few moments to observe us. Then, leaping and bounding, it had vanished behind the crevice of a rock. Angmo had taken out the food she had prepared to take to the festival and we had eaten together. How quiet it had been after that! The sky above and Angmo and me below! No other living soul in sight.

I thought I located the spot where the chorten must have stood but all around me there were only houses. There could be a reasonable explanation for the missing rock, I told myself. Someone could have broken it and used the stone to build a house. But where could the chorten have gone? Despondently, I followed the path and continued my search. Tourists were making their way down after visiting the palace and monastery. I wandered until I reached a large market teeming with crowds and cars. The shops were filled with food and other goods. Peddlers and vegetable sellers were sitting on the pavement, their wares displayed in front. Seeing this mass of people, memories of another crowded day in Leh overtook me.

There had been a fair in Leh town. It was there that I had first seen Angmo and had lost my heart at first sight.

"Who is that girl?" I had nudged the man beside me as though waking up from a dream.

"That one who has the tiny child in her lap?"

"No, not she."

"The one with the blue velvet hat?"

"No." I said in exasperation. How could he not know whom I meant?

"The one who is resting her chin on her hand and watching the show?"

"Yes, that one."

"She's Angmo, the daughter of the headman. Isn't she beautiful?"

"Her mannerisms are exquisite." I spoke reluctantly.

After that encounter, I had waited for hours outside her house in the biting cold just to catch a glimpse of her beauty, until one day when she acknowledged me and agreed to meet at the rock in front of the chorten.

I walked towards the steps that were carved into the dark and narrow ravine. It was said that the craggy sinews of this ravine could exhaust both humans and horses alike. I climbed the mountain steps to the magnificent monastery and gazed into the open valley. Housing colonies could be seen all around. I looked at the numerous cars on the road. This place was overflowing with wealth. Angmo and I had possessed so little.

She had married me despite objections of her family. "Don't be foolish, Angmo," her father had reprimanded. "He doesn't even have a proper house to live in. Just a handful of earth. Humans can't live on love alone." But poverty could not burst our bubble of joy. Life was so radiant those days.

I gazed at the panorama around me for a while and then descended on the trail that Angmo and I had walked forty years ago. I wished I could rest my tired head against this earth, stamped with the traces of our youthful footsteps. There used to be such solitude here, such peace. Sometimes progress can be so disastrous. At that time, there was nothing here except a well-known saying that in this valley, witches run wild and fly high on long, wooden beams.

The young man: "What are you looking for, Memeley?" I asked, unable to stop staring at him. How strange his attire was and how odd his behaviour! I had seen him descend from the bus yesterday, bathed in the evening light. He was a source of curiosity, a giant question mark for all the pedestrians between the bus station and the bazaar. A desire had risen in our hearts to find out who he was, what his name was, where he had come from, and where he was going. A group of children had followed him, yelling, "Madman! Madman!" I had admonished them and tried to chase them away but they had dispersed only for a few moments before gathering again. Before I could summon the courage to approach him, he had disappeared.

Now, here he was, in this alley on the way to my house.

"There used to be a chorten somewhere here at one time ..." He murmured in a confused manner.

"What time are you talking about?" I asked.

"Forty years ago."

I couldn't help smiling. "I wasn't even born then. Where have you come from, Memeley?"

"I'm a resident of Leh, my son. I'm returning home after forty years but everything is so different that I feel completely lost."

"Like Rip Van Winkle?"

"What is that?"

"It's the name of a man. We learned about him in our seventh standard textbook. He returns home after many years. He doesn't know the town and the town folk do not recognize him. Why are you looking for this chorten now, Memeley?"

He heaved a long sigh and said, "It's a long story, Nono. If we meet again and you have the time, then I will tell you in detail. Are you from Leh?"

"I'm from Chang Thang originally. My name is Dawa Tshering. It's been five years since we settled in Leh."

"Do people from Chang Thang live here?" The old man was amazed.

"Memeley, you will find people from Chang Thang, Zangskar, Sham, Nubra, and Kargil who have come to Leh and settled here. There are Kashmiris, people from Down, and even foreigners."

"I had heard that in the days of the kings, representatives from different villages would come to Leh in winter and stay within the palace gates for one or two months. Now you are telling me that people from all parts of Ladakh come to Leh to settle down." He shook his head in disbelief and walked ahead.

Suddenly a thought occurred to me. "Memeley," I called out to him. "Now I remember. They say that some chortens were transferred to some other place when they were building the roads and offices here." The old man nodded. Hope flickered in his eyes.

"Please Memeley, won't you tell me why you are searching so?"

He put down his sack. "If you must know, Nono Dawa. I will tell you a story."

I looked up at the blue sky and the palace facade. I felt as if I was in a magical world. The afternoon had taken a strangely gratifying turn.

"There once was a prosperous and successful trader in the village of Saspol," the old man began. His voice was sombre and seemed to come from far away. "The only child of his parents. One day, the young trader saw an orphaned baby sparrow perched on a tree, downy feathers sprouting on its body. The sensitive youth contemplated the life of this bird. It seemed to him that the bird did not suffer from the death of its father. If he too were to renounce his home to become a monk, it would not affect his family. Thus, forsaking his house and family, like the Buddha Sakyamuni, he went to Tholing in Western Tibet and became a monk. From Tholing, he went to Tashigang to attend the assembly of the great Rimpoche. Next, he went to meditate at Lake Manasarovar. He lived only on barley and water.

"One day, he saw smoke rising from below, from the camps near the shore of the lake. When he went to the lake to draw water, he found some people who had come from Ladakh. On a pilgrimage, you see. Among them was his sister, Garmo. Seeing her brother in these torn, ragged clothes, Garmo wept a lot. She begged him to return to Ladakh but he did not agree. Then she pleaded with him to accompany her to Tholing where she requested the great Rimpoche to instruct his disciple to return to Ladakh. Her request was granted. The teacher decreed that his student's field of duty would be Ladakh. So the man returned to Ladakh where he met other monks and later established the monastery of …"

"Rizong. He was the founder of Rizong monastery, wasn't he?" Somehow the words came to my lips but even though I tried, I couldn't remember the name of the man in the story. I had been reading about the history and architecture of Ladakh, hoping to find work as a tourist guide with Paradise Tours in the summer. The previous summer, I had led two trekking groups, one to see the wildlife and lakes of Chang Thang and the other to the monasteries in Sham. All the tourists seemed enchanted with the unspoiled, untamed nature of Ladakh. I realized that I would have to learn so much more about our history to do well in my profession. I wanted to know about the old man's world. I could tell that he had a lot to teach me.

But my question remained unanswered.

"The sun is setting, Nono. I have matters that I must tend to."

I watched him leave, turning his rosary and chanting mantras. I decided to look for him another day.

The friend: I recognized him at once despite those unruly tresses and filthy garb. There was something in his eyes and gait that was as familiar as my own shadow. He was wandering down the main street, my closest friend, whom I hadn't seen in forty years. I strode up to him and paused.

"Phuntsog Tashi?" I inquired, even though I had no doubt in my mind about who he was.

"Do I know you?" My toothless and wrinkled face must have puzzled him.

"It's me, Dawa ... Dawa Norbu."

He almost leapt on me and clutched me in a tight embrace. Our eyes were moist with tears. We had so many years to catch up with. He told me about the places he had visited and the burdens he had borne, of how he had become a monk and travelled to Western Tibet. He told me how he had been to Lake Manosarovar and then made his way to Tholing where he had sat meditating for several years in a dark cave. At that time, the Communists had already taken over Tibet but the Dalai Lama still lived there and no prohibition had yet been levied on Ladakhis entering the region for trade or pilgrimage.

From Western Tibet, he had travelled to Central Tibet. When conditions deteriorated in Tibet, he fled with other Tibetans and reached Nepal where he meditated in a monastery for a number of years.

I was mesmerized by his tales. I could hardly believe that he was standing before me. He had been inconsolable after Angmo died in childbirth. I had been worried that he would do something drastic. He hadn't been capable of taking care of Sonam, his son. If his sister Dolma hadn't helped, things would have surely fallen apart. As children, we had read the biography of Kushok Tshultim Nyima, the founder of Rizong monastery, who had renounced his worldly life in his quest for spiritual peace. Phuntsog had become obsessed with the idea of meditating like Tshultim Nyima. Expressing his desire to Dolma, he had told her that this town was gnawing at him. Dolma could not stand to see her brother's anguish and had taken charge of the newborn baby.

"What about children? And grandchildren?" he asked, still postponing the inevitable question.

"I have two sons, Lhundup and Angchug. Angchug is a storekeeper. He has done well for himself. Lhundup runs a big hotel called Lha-yul and a travel agency and even maintains two tippers."

"You are fortunate. The gods have graced your house." He fell quiet.

"And Sonam?" Finally he uttered the name that had been on his lips all along.

"Sonam has made a lot of progress. He now owns a big hotel and also runs a travel agency."

Phuntsog's eyes shone.

"It's not our world any more, Phuntsog, the new age is different. We were poor," I said, as we walked towards their house on Old Fort Road.

"Memeley, who is this cartoon you are bringing here?" Sonam's son, Tashi, came up to us.

"Don't talk like this, son, he is your …"

I saw Sonam approach.

"… Memeley." I finished my sentence.

I watched Sonam freeze in the doorway. For him, his father had passed away a long time ago. The past had taken a severe toll on him. After his aunt Dolma's death, he had driven himself like a machine to make sure life brought him nothing but success.

Sonam quickly recovered his composure and instructed his children to greet their grandfather. I left Phuntsog with his family, promising to return the next day. I did not tell him then that even though I tried to maintain close ties with Sonam, the relations between our families were strained due to suspicion, rivalry, and bitterness.

The next morning, he came over at the crack of dawn. He had seen pictures of Angmo which had released a flood of memories. We spent hours talking.

One day, at Lhundup's urging, I told Phuntsog that we needed a small fragment of their land for a path from our hotel to the main street. Phuntsog said he would talk to Sonam but I knew it would be futile.

Another evening, as we were sitting on the terrace, basking in the sun, eating apricot seeds and reminiscing our childhood, we heard loud voices quarrelling.

Lhundup was shouting. "Sonam, why are you defaming our hotel?"

"The thief yelling at the warden? That's great. It is you who misleads the tourists coming to our hotel and takes them to your hotel."

"No, you are the thief. What did you tell the tourists about us the other day? Bedbugs? Dirty Water? Cheats?"

"And what did you tell the tourists last month? Have you forgotten so soon? That we fill the water tank with dirty stream water? As though you use clear, spring water."

"Don't bark at me."

"May your enemies bark."

"You can't bear to see our hotel prosper."

"You can make ten hotels. Why should I be jealous?"

"Beware, Sonam! If, in the future, you spread rumours about our hotel, the consequences will not be pleasant."

Sonam said something in reply but we could not catch it. Their voices became faint and a silence spread all around. I could see tears shining in Phuntsog's eyes.

"Today's children are not like us, Phuntsog." I tried to ease the deep tension lurking in the air. "We would share even a bulb of onion or a cup of sugar or a slice of bread. Do you remember, Phuntsog, once, when my goat died, you and Angmo came home to give me moral support? The children of today do not even have time to greet each other."

One night, I was awakened from sleep. Kunzes, Phuntsog's daughter-in-law, was screaming that people from our house had released water into their compound, causing their wall to collapse. Hearing the noise, Lhundup and his wife started for

Sonam's house. I shuffled behind them with my stick and stood in the shadows.

"What has happened?" Lhundup asked anxiously.

"Why don't you ask what has not happened?" Sonam replied harshly.

"We did not release the water on purpose, Sonam." Lhundup tried to make peace. "Last night, water overflowed in the canal. There is water swamping our vegetable gardens too. Please don't cry. We will build you a new wall."

"It is not a question of a new wall," Sonam was furious and unmoving. "Today, you released the water and demolished the garden wall. Tomorrow, you can demolish the house. Then our hotel the day after."

"As the Three Jewels, the Buddha, Dharma, and Sangha, are our witnesses, we have not done this on purpose, Sonam." Lhundup's wife implored.

Just then a policeman came in with some of Sonam's employees and the situation took a turn for the worse.

"You have called the police, Sonam?" Lhundup's voice had lost its conciliatory tone. "Until today no policeman has ever entered our neighbourhood. What can the police do? Don't think you are going to frighten us like this."

"Did you see him deliberately release the water?" the Head Constable asked.

"How will darkness be visible in daylight?" retorted Sonam. Lhundup pleaded innocence.

"This is a matter to be resolved between two neighbours," declared the Constable. "You sort it out. The report hasn't been registered yet. If the case reaches the court, it will be a long drawn issue."

I could not stay quiet anymore. I had to intervene. I walked in and beseeched the constable to leave. Then turning to Sonam, I said, "We are deeply sorry that the water from our garden has destroyed your wall. I have come to apologize. Tell me what the damages are. I will pay it."

"We will pay nothing, Aba. He has called the police. Two can play this game."

"No. We will pay, Lhundup," I insisted.

Just then, Phuntsog stepped out. "What are you saying, Dawa Norbu? We don't want anything. We value our neighbours more."

"Aba, you go inside," ordered Sonam. "This ruse is beyond your understanding."

"You are the schemer," accused Lhundup.

"No, you are."

Lhundup and Sonam almost came to blows and we had to drag them apart. It was a disturbing night. It left our hearts heavy.

Phuntsog took this incident very badly. He began spending most of his time with me outside the city limits where the chorten he and Angmo loved used to stand.

"If only I still had my hovel," he would lament. "I would hide in it and reminisce about the year Angmo and I spent with such love and happiness. I would sit by the patch from which Angmo tended the hearth. I would touch the kitchen shelves that Angmo's hands had touched. I would stick my head out of the window from which she peered when I called out to her."

My own life had been content in many respects. I had only a few regrets about the past. As I listened to him, I wished he could compromise with time too.

The son: "Aba," I said to him, this man with whom the bones of my existence were linked, "I had hoped against hope that you would return to us to see how well your son has fared."

I introduced him to my wife, Kunzes, and children – Tashi, who helped me at work, and Jigmed and Dolkar, who were home on their summer vacation from their school in Mussourie.

"Why did you stay away for so long, Memeley?" asked Tashi. I wondered what answer he would have for this question.

"When your grandmother passed away, this land became unbearable for me, Nono."

"Did you ever think of us?"

"All the time. In Nepal, I heard from a monk that you all were very successful. My heart swelled with pride."

"Did you also hear that Ane Dolma died ten years ago?" I couldn't resist asking.

"I did, son. It will have to be in a future life that I can repay all the debts I owe her. What a fine family she raised in my absence."

"Aba," I said, when it grew late, "You should rest a little. Tomorrow you will see our hotel. We will get you decent clothes. And do something about those hermit-like long locks. I'll bring a barber home."

He was adamant about not cutting his hair although he did put on the new set of clothes I gave him. We walked to my hotel, an imposing building of cement and stones that I had named Shangri-la Palace. In the garden in front, bare white bodies were tanning themselves under the sun.

"This is a group that has come from France to trek in the remote and rugged Himalayan landscape," I told him.

I checked on a few things with Dawa Tshering, the young tour guide I had hired the day before. Oddly, Aba seemed to know him but I did not have time to linger. I walked with Aba to the main bazaar and showed him the three shops I owned, each of which brought me forty thousand rupees in rent. I was planning on increasing the rent by five thousand next year.

"Forty thousand rupees is a lot of money, Sonam." Aba didn't agree with the idea.

"There are Kashmiris who are ready to pay forty five thousand per shop, Abaley. It is not I who has imposed these prices on my own. A good businessman has to move with the times."

He was quiet and seemed lost in his thoughts.

"Abaley," I asked as we walked along, "How much did you sell our ancestral field for?"

"Three hundred rupees, Nono."

A sigh escaped me. "Today, one can't even pay ten lakhs to purchase such a property in this area."

"Those days land was very cheap, Sonam. In this place especially. It wasn't considered that valuable."

"Aba, you really shouldn't have sold that kanal of land. Today its value would have reached the sky."

"Those days were different, son. We had no place to cover our heads. So your mother and I sold some of our land and built a home."

"You built a hovel, Aba."

"What did you do with that hovel?" He looked anxious.

What could I do with it? I had razed it to the ground. And built a hotel room or a bathroom in its place.

When I related this to him, I noticed the panic-stricken look in his eyes.

The street was teeming with people. We stopped by a restaurant where several tourists were gathered.

"Aba," I pointed out, "The land you sold – this restaurant is built on that very stretch. The owner had no trouble leasing it out. The person who leased it invested his own money to fix it. They have an agreement that he won't rent this space to anyone else. He's paying eighty thousand rupees a year in rent. Do you know how much business the restaurants do? Ten thousand rupees a day. During the last three to four years, this man has earned lakhs of rupees in profit."

A client came up to me with a smile. I shook hands with him warmly and introduced him to my father.

"This man is from Germany. He has come here to experience the solitude of the mountains and has been staying in our hotel for the last month. Now, if only that property was still with us, I could accommodate so many other visitors like him."

"I told you how we had to sell that land to make a house, Nono. Who knew that this property would have been so valuable one day?"

Aba did not seem to appreciate my business sense. As though I didn't have a right to question him about the land of our forefathers. He had no idea about the taunts and pitying glances I had endured for most of my life. He had no idea of modern times, of the needs of children, of progress in society.

What irked me most was his sympathy for my competitors. He argued that Dawa Norbu was his oldest friend and a kind neighbour. I explained how our business had suffered adversely because of their family. How his two sons had filled our lives with poison. How they had copied every move we made. When we bought a car, they also bought a car. We opened a travel business so they did the same, drastically undercutting our profits for a year. Then, we built a hotel, so they also built one. We ran shops, so they too ran shops. I had applied for a contract for a cooking gas agency. Tomorrow, if it were to be accepted, I'm sure they would stick their foot in that as well. I had purchased an acre of land to build a factory for chopping firewood. Tomorrow, they could copy that too. And who knows what else!

But Aba defended Dawa Norbu and his brood by saying, "What's wrong with that? If they do it, let them. Your work is going well, isn't it? In the future also, I pray that it will run smoothly. God has given you so much, Sonam. What else do you want? Dawa Norbu was a very good neighbour."

In every house, there is need of a worldly man. If there had been a worldly wise man in our house, I would not have had to face the struggle with modern times all alone. How could someone, cut off from society for most of his life, know the demands and obligations of that society!

One day, the wily Lhundup even put him up to making me sell them land for a pathway to their hotel. He fell right into Lhundup's trap and accused me unjustly.

"Do you know that they have no way to get to the hotel? Lhundup says that he has requested you several times but you have not even responded. They are prepared to give you whatever sum of money you ask for. If you want land in exchange, they will give you property three times the size in another place."

I stood my ground. "Even if he gives me bricks of gold, I will not give him the land. I do not wish to drop an axe on my foot, Aba. Lhundup is building a hotel and shopping complex. It is good to keep him in check."

The old man looked confused but continued to lecture me on this issue that was beyond his understanding. "Sonam, you must have heard of the proverb that an enemy nearby is better than a relative far away. One day we will also require their assistance."

My heart was sore with his betrayal.

The one person Aba seemed to open up to was my daughter, Dolkar. He found her adorable. Perhaps he saw Ama's reflection in her. People often commented how Dolkar was a spitting image of Ama. Dolkar liked to listen to stories of the past. They were very quaint to her. Aba told her tales of his childhood. He told her that when he was a child there was no electricity in Leh, no phones in the houses, no television or radio. He said this as if it was a virtue.

"We used to walk barefoot," he would begin, sipping a hot cup of butter tea. "Our clothes had patches on them. Rising early in the morning, we would take a basket to collect cowdung. Occasionally, we would go to school. Or else our parents would send us to graze the sheep and goats."

"Till what class have you studied, Memeley?"

"Till the third standard."

Dolkar giggled. "I'm in the fourth standard now."

"I'm one class ahead of Memeley," she told her mother.

"So what did you do when you grew up, Memeley?"

"I used to travel as a begar labourer. This was a system of forced labour imposed on Ladakhis by the colonial administration. When big officers came to Leh, we had to carry their wives and children from one place to another in a palanquin. I prepared horses for their journey. We had to sit outside the contractor's place for a meagre livelihood. At the end of it all, he would take his own cut from us."

"Was there no government?" I asked.

"Those days we used to tremble in fear at even the name of the government. When landlords and moneylenders gave us grain on loan, they charged an exorbitant interest if it was not repaid in time. Once a farmer took a loan from a money lender to buy an electricity."

"How does one buy *an* electricity, Memeley?" Dolkar chirped.

"There is an electricity right next to you.".

"Memeley, this is a torch."

"We used to call it bijli, electricity. As I was saying, a farmer took a loan to buy one. He could not pay back the loan on time and the lender charged him such a high rate of interest that he had to wash his hands off his field. The field still exists and is called Bijli field."

It seemed as if his mind was a storeroom of stories about why things had been named as they were. Sometimes, I worried about his preoccupation , that he was oblivious to the changes in the world around him.

The summer holidays ended and the children returned to their schools. Without Dolkar, Aba seemed lonelier. He was withdrawn and melancholic. He would reply to our questions in very few words. He ate with difficulty. His health deteriorated. He began to spend most of his time outside the house. The distance between us widened more than in all those years when he was away. We were like strangers to one another. As if his return had cost me my father.

One day, when I woke up in the morning, he was packing his old clothes and things in his sack.

"What are you doing so early in the morning?" I asked.

"I am going."

"Going where?" I was astonished.

"I'm not sure. But I am going, Sonam."

My wife and I tried hard to stop him but he did not listen and picking up his sack, left my house. I watched as he vanished from sight, wondering whether I would see him again, helpless to reach over the cold wall that had grown so tall between us.

A MAN OF INFLUENCE

No one's coming out," groaned the man in the queue, straining his neck to survey the counter.

"Some idiot must be sitting there! People have such slow hands!" The person standing behind quickly jumped in.

"Some folks bring four-four, five-five forms to deposit money," grumbled a short man waiting behind them.

"I hear they have their own people who get work done through a secret thieves' window," said the first man.

"Not a thieves' window, a thieves' *door*," refuted the second.

"It's the same thing, whether you call it a window or a door. It's robbery, all the same."

All of a sudden, there was a ruckus at the counter.

"What kind of chaos is this?" The first man in the queue shouted. "We've been waiting for one whole hour and you are continuously passing forms from behind."

There was a ripple in the queue as the others listened attentively. The clerk's reply was not audible at the back but the man standing before him bellowed loud and clear. "We have work too. Our time is precious too. You have already obliged ten people so far by saying you will just do one or two."

"That young man is right." There was no dearth of supporters.

"There's always a crowd during the first month. They should have opened two counters for this period," observed Ghulam Mohammed, who had been standing in the queue for a long, long time, quietly listening to the conversation.

Just then, from the corner of his eye, Ghulam Mohammed noticed Jameel enter the bank. Jameel cast a fleeting glance at the queue as he walked in through the door near the last counter. He went over to the bukhari in the middle of the room and warmed his hands for a few minutes.

The young man at the counter deposited his money, took his receipt and moved away. The queue inched forward.

"They too are responsible for the long line," griped the short man softly, pointing to the soldiers and paramilitary personnel standing in the queue.

As he walked towards the door, the man who had just left the queue addressed one soldier. "Soldier Saheb, don't you have a bank in your camp?"

"If there was one, why would we come here?" The soldier replied harshly.

The queue moved forward slowly. New arrivals extended the line which now meandered all the way to the stairs. A few women had formed a rather disorderly parallel line by the counter.

Ghulam Mohammed reached an angle in the queue from where he could see Jameel sipping tea with some of the bank staff. A thin wisp of smoke was rising from their teacups. Outside, the temperature was below freezing point and the sky was overcast. Smouldering coals in the bukharis had heated up the interior of the bank.

Ghulam Mohammed stared at Jameel in envy and waited apprehensively for Jameel to notice him. There was a slight push in the queue as one man made space for another beside him. The people behind protested but the man did not budge. When Ghulam Mohammed looked back at the counter, Jameel had left. He cast another glance at his watch. It was quarter past twelve. He had been standing in the line since eleven o'clock but there were still six men ahead of him. A few minutes later he saw Jameel again, chatting casually with a staff member who then said something to a guard. The guard took a blue form from the counter and gave it to him. He filled it up and gave it to Jameel who took a pen and probably signed his name on the form. The staff member disappeared from the counter, reappearing in a few minutes to hand over the receipt to a clerk.

Now there were only three men before Ghulam Mohammed. The clerk found an error in one man's form and instructed him to fill another.

Thank God, one man less! Ghulam Mohammed felt some elation but the very next moment he regretted his pleasure. After all, this thin and weak looking man had also been standing in the line for the last hour and a half.

"Acho Ghulam," Jameel's voice came from behind the counter. "Congratulations! Here to increase your bank balance, are you?"

"I have to make a draft, my friend."

"Where do you need to send it?" Jameel drew closer.

"To Arshad. I have to send it through someone. The flight to Jammu leaves the day after tomorrow. Haven't found anyone I know as yet but if there's someone trustworthy, I'll send it through him rather than the post. I have been standing in the line for a mere thousand rupees since eleven o'clock. My legs are aching from exhaustion."

"Give me your form. I'll get the draft made." Jameel held out his hand.

"There are just two men left. It's my turn after them."

"I've come into the bank twice myself. The first time to withdraw some cash and now to make a draft."

"Has it been made?"

"Yes."

"Jameel, please do me a favour," Ghulam Mohammed suddenly remembered. "I have to get two air tickets to Srinagar confirmed."

"Two? For whom?"

"For Razia and me. The doctor has referred Razia's case to the Srinagar Medical Institute."

"Achey hasn't recovered yet?"

"No, the doctor had given a letter of recommendation for the airlines manager to issue priority tickets but the manager rejected it saying there were no spare seats."

"He's talking rubbish. They have lots of seats."

"I begged and pleaded that I'm not travelling for pleasure. The Leh-Srinagar road is closed. I have an aged patient with me. But this had no effect on him. My pleas fell on deaf ears."

"No problem! I will get it done."

"They said the computer isn't working."

"It's just an excuse."

"I have the tickets with me." Ghulam Mohammed took out the tickets from his shirt pocket. "We're on the waiting list. Number one fifty and one fifty one."

"This is not a difficult task," Jameel took the tickets. "If necessary, I will tell Mr Morup and get them okayed." His voice was very confident.

"I will be indebted to you."

Ghulam Mohammed reached the counter and placed his form and money on it. Just then, the man who had been turned away pushed his form forward and reminded Ghulam Mohammed that he had been in the queue before him.

Ghulam Mohammed quietly gave him the spot in front.

Jameel called as he left, "Ghulam Mohammed, can you come to my house tomorrow? I have an important matter to discuss with you."

Ghulam Mohammed placed the form and money at the counter once again. A hand from behind slipped a rolled form into the thin holes. To make the clerk aware of his presence, Ghulam Mohammed moved his form and currency notes toward the opening but the clerk did not even bat an eyelid to acknowledge him as he took the rolled up form passed from behind. Ghulam Mohammed did not utter a word in protest. He was happy that his meeting with Jameel was successful. He was surprised at himself for not having thought of Jameel until today. At one time, both of them had worked together. After completing their schooling, they had both managed to get positions as clerks. Over the years, Jameel had been promoted all the way to the post of office superintendent. Then he had become head clerk. He had retired two months ago, and entered politics a few days later. He was ahead of Ghulam Mohammed in every thing and was especially clever at getting his work done. Ghulam Mohammed had never been able to compete against him. Once Jameel had even called him Stupid. Age makes one forget a lot of things but he had never been able to forget this insult.

After depositing his money, he went to another counter to request for a draft. The clerk concerned asked him to return at three o'clock to collect it. His eyes involuntarily fell on his watch. It was almost half past one.

Ghulam Mohammed quickly made his way home. When he reached the street corner, a newly constructed black wall loomed in front like a demon. His heart ached at the sight. He was angry at his carelessness for he had come this way several times by mistake. He turned back and taking the roundabout route by the bridge, walked towards his home.

The next day, he went to visit Jameel and found out that he had confirmed his airline reservations. Ghulam Mohammed's face glowed with happiness.

"You've done wonders, my friend! I tried endlessly but nothing came of it."

"Being straight gets you nowhere. Lots of flour has to be kneaded for a loaf of bread." Jameel said smugly.

"My General Provident fund hasn't been released yet. I will go to Srinagar and find out about this. What times these are! We have to give bribes to withdraw our own savings."

"Indeed, the old values and feelings of fellowship have all disappeared," agreed Jameel.

"Jameel, did you know that the old path to our neighbourhood has been closed off?"

"By whom?"

"Khan Saheb. My forefathers' footprints are imprinted on that sidewalk. All my life, I have walked that path to enter and leave home. Now I am over sixty four years old. The road used by generations before me has been closed in one night."

"Haven't you done anything about it?"

"People of our neighbourhood have written an application. Twenty days have passed but no action has been taken. We fear that this case may come to the same end as the other illegally closed roads in this area."

"You must have to take a detour," Jameel said sympathetically.

"Yes, I take the old footpath and go towards the edge of the bridge. Then I reach the back of the alley. That place has piles of rubbish. The whole neighbourhood throws its garbage there."

After a pause, Ghulam Mohammed said, "I've heard that there is a law stipulating that a road on which people have walked for three years cannot be closed. Jameel, why doesn't the justice system do its work?"

"Khan Saheb is very cunning and his hands are very long," replied Jameel.

"Are they longer than the law?"

"The law is powerful beyond limits but when those who run it are weak, then even the law is helpless before long hands. The problem is that you have no influential person in your neighbourhood."

"What can a man with influence do?" asked Ghulam Mohammed, a little surprised.

"Ghulam, you are naive, like always."

"Call me stupid, my friend."

Jameel laughed. "It seems you still haven't forgotten that. Ghulam, water taps don't run dry, electric lights are not turned off in a community that has an influential and charismatic man. Rather, there are private faucets and special electric connections in his house. Do you understand?"

Observing Ghulam Mohammed's silence, Jameel continued. "We will think about the road issue later. I have called you to my house to discuss something important."

Ghulam Mohammed gazed at Jameel curiously.

"Why don't you enter politics? Join our party!"

"Me and politics?" It was Ghulam Mohommed's turn to laugh. "I have no status."

"Why do you think that? You are regarded as an upright man, both by the people in your community and neighbouring ones. They listen to you. You must have heard that the assembly election is going to take place soon. We need men like you."

"Jameel, isn't it better for us to stay away from such intrigues at our age?"

"It may be better but what are we to do about these problems that surround us – like your road problem, your air ticket problem, the problem of Razia's treatment? The problem of admitting her into the medical institute when you take her to Srinagar. For this, you probably need a recommendation. When Arshad returns after graduation, there will be the problem of his employment. Jobs are not handed out on a platter."

"Is there no end to our problems and helplessness? Will Arshad get a job by my entering politics?"

"It's not guaranteed but it can at least be a step towards it. Besides, you are talking as if you have to climb a mountain. During the election month, you have to do some work for the party. That's all. After that, there is only enjoyment. Look at our current leaders! They don't even stay here beyond a few months in the summer."

Jameel raised his voice righteously. "Ghulam Mohammed, it is not written in your destiny or mine whether we will become leaders, but can't we at least lead the way in the search for one? Do you know why I entered politics?"

Ghulam Mohammed observed Jameel's face silently.

"You know that there was an explosion in town. The police arrested Afzal and some other boys and thrashed them soundly. That day, our house was like a morgue. Afzal's mother's condition was pitiful. At twelve in the night, Morup Saheb called the police station and got Afzal released. I've been in his party ever since."

Both men were quiet for some time. After a few moments, Jameel confided, "I've heard that this time also Morup Saheb will be given the party ticket."

"Couldn't you get a better candidate?"

"What do you mean by Better?"

"People have become very conscious now. Perhaps many won't even vote for Morup Saheb."

"If people are clever, we have to be cleverer. If they are discerning, we have to be more discerning. That's what successful politics is."

Ghulam Mohammed did not utter a word.

Jameel carried on. "When you return from Srinagar, the election date will have been announced."

Three days later, the evening news bulletin of the local radio station announced that Ghulam Mohammed had been admitted into the Working Committee of the National Unity Party.

Ghulam Mohammed and Razia returned from Srinagar after a month. Razia's health had improved. Walking along the footpath, they came to the edge of the bridge from where they reached the back of the alley. They were astonished to see that there was no garbage or rubbish. The road was clear and shining, like a mirror. Houses had been whitewashed. On both sides of the street, blue and yellow pieces of paper, tied with strings, were merrily flapping in the wind.

"We aren't dreaming, are we?" Razia asked in amazement.

"Hey, Nono, what's the matter? Why is everything so different?" Ghulam Mohammed inquired of a pedestrian.

"The Governor passed by the day before yesterday to lay the foundation stone for the industrial centre."

Ghulam Mohammed muttered, "Razia, if only the Governor would pass by once a year!"

The election date had been fixed and the candidates had filed their nomination papers. Election campaigns started. There were three candidates in the fray besides Morup Saheb.

Ghulam Mohammed gathered people from his neighbourhood and appealed to them to give their precious votes to Morup Saheb, his Party's candidate.

The people told him that in the last election too they had voted for Morup Saheb but he had never shown his face after winning. Their community tap worked for only four months, electricity played hide and seek and the road had been closed off. They rejected Morup Saheb's candidacy straight away.

"Give him another chance," implored Ghulam Mohammed. "He is standing on the Party ticket. It is only this Party that has the capacity to come into power and so it is to our advantage to support Morup Saheb. He will himself come to meet us. You can all place your complaints before him. You can lay your demands before him. I will also speak to him and make him aware of your concerns. He will definitely pay attention to your complaints."

"Under no circumstance will we agree to meet him," they shouted in unison.

An old man addressed Ghulam Mohammed. "We did not expect such a man as you to lead us along a fool's path."

Ghulam Mohammed felt the ground slip from under his feet. His throat dried up and he licked his lips in distress.

Three days later, from the local radio station, it was relayed that Ghulam Mohammed had been expelled from the membership of the National Unity Party for anti-party activities and for not supporting its candidate.

That evening, walking back from a long wait at the bank, Ghulam Mohammed absent-mindedly followed the old route to his house. The black wall loomed before him. Strangely, it did not torment him today. He shook his head ruefully at his mistake and took the long way home.

ABDUL GHANI SHEIKH wrote his first story while he was a veterinarian stock assistant in Srinagar. He has worked as a schoolteacher, screenplay writer and journalist. Changes wrought by development are recurrent themes in his writings. With psychological intuition, his stories probe the social problems of common people coping with a world in which justice is not always the outcome of action and are pragmatic, ironic and tinged with realism.

Recognized as one of the foremost scholars of Ladakh, Abdul Ghani Sheikh has, apart from creative fiction, written on varied subjects – literature, history, philosophy and comparative religion. Among his books are two collections of short stories, *Zojila Ke Aar Paar* and *Do Raha*, a biography on the famous Ladakhi pioneer, Sonam Norbu, a historical novel *Woh Zamana* and a romantic novel *Dil Hi To Hai*, which won the Jammu and Kashmir Cultural Academy's Best Book Award. His non-fictional books, *Ladakh ki Kahani* and *Kitabon ki Duniya*, won second and third place in a State competition held for the Children's Centenary Year in 1986.

RAVINA AGGARWAL who teaches anthropology at Smith College, Massachusetts has been actively interested and involved in the Himalayan district of Ladakh which she has been visiting and writing about since 1989. Over the last twelve years, she has explored the connection between social space and nationalism in this Himalayan district. Her research has focused on political history, cultural performances, gender roles, and education of the region and she has written extensively on Ladakhi political history and expressive culture. She has tried to show how local writing reflects the dilemmas of development and how literature can be mobilized to affect policy and practice. She also runs a Non Government Organization concerned with literacy and development in Ladakh.

KATHA TRAILBLAZER SERIES

Paul Zacharia
Paul Zacharia: Two Novellas
Translated by Gita Krishanankutty
Malayalam Library/Fiction

Ashokamitran
Water
Translated by Lakshmi Holmstrom
Tamil Library/Fiction

FORTHCOMING TITLES

Bhupen Khakhar
Two Stories and a Novella
Translated by Bina Srinivasan, Ganesh Devy and
Naushil Mehta
Gujarati Library/Fiction

Indira Goswami
Pages Stained with Blood
Translated by Pradeep Acharya
Asomiya Library/Fiction

ABOUT KATHA

A nonprofit organization, Katha endeavours to spread the joy of reading, knowing, and living amongst adults and children, the common reader and the neo-literate. Katha's main objective is **to enhance the pleasures of reading for children and adults**, for experienced readers as well as for those who are just beginning to read. And, inter alia, to –

- Stimulate an interest in lifelong learning that will help the child grow into a confident, self-reliant, responsible and responsive adult.
- Help break down gender, cultural and social stereotypes.
- Encourage, foster excellence, and applaud quality literature and translations in and between the various Indian languages.

A QUICK LOOK AT KATHA'S WORK
KALPAVRIKSHAM: The Centre for Sustainable Learning

- **Kalpana**: Nonformal Education Resource Centre (Tamasha!; Teacher training; T/L materials development)
- **KATHA KHAZANA: A learning centre for one of Delhi's largest slum clusters in Govindpuri** The components in this programme are:
- **The Katha School of Entrepreneurship:** (1300 children, 0 – 17 years of age)
- **Shakti Khazana**: the women's empowerment & income-generation programme
- **Saat Sahelia:** Post literacy material development & publishing programme

KATHA VILASAM: The Story & Translation Research & Resource Centre was begun in 1989 and has seen steady growth and development in terms of ideas and vision. It consists of –

- **Katha Books**: Publishing of Quality Translations under various series
- **Academic Publishing Programme:** Books for teaching of translation and Indian fiction
- **Applauding Excellence**: The Katha Awards for fiction, translation, editing
- **Kathakaar**: The Centre for Children's Literature
- **Katha Barani**: The Translation Resource Centre
- **Katha Sethu**: Building bridges between India and the outside world
  - **The Katha Translation Exchange Programme**
  - **Translation Contests**

KATHA SCHOOL OF TRANSLATION AND INNOVATIVE EDUCATION was started in 1994 with the Vak Initiative for enhancing the pool of translators between the various bhashas.

- **Katha Academic Centres**. In various universities across the country
- **The Faculty Enhancement programme**. Workshops, seminars, discussions
- **Sishya:** Katha Clubs in colleges; workshops, certificate courses, events and contests
- **The Katha Internship programme** for students from outside India
- **The Friends of Katha Network** with its more than 3,000 volunteers.

Be a Friend of Katha!

If you feel strongly about Indian literature, you belong with us! KathaNet, an invaluable network of our friends, is the mainstay of all our translation-related activities. We are happy to invite you to join this ever-widening circle of translation activists. Katha, with limited financial resources, is propped up by the unqualified enthusiasm and the indispensable support of nearly 5000 dedicated women and men.

We are constantly on the lookout for people who can spare the time to find stories for us, and to translate them. Katha has been able to access mainly the literature of the major Indian languages. Our efforts to locate resource people who could make the lesser-known literatures available to us have not yielded satisfactory results. We are specially eager to find Friends who could introduce us to Bhojpuri, Dogri, Kashmiri, Maithili, Manipuri, Nepali, Rajasthani and Sindhi fiction.

Do write to us with details about yourself, your language skills, the ways in which you can help us, and any material that you already have and feel might be publishable under a Katha programme. All this would be a labour of love, of course! But we do offer a discount of 20% on all our publications to Friends of Katha.

Write to us at –
Katha
A-3 Sarvodaya Enclave
Sri Aurobindo Marg
New Delhi 110 017   Or call us at: 652 4511, 652 4350